# The force of the blast sent Declan flying backward against the pavement.

The breath was knocked from his lungs and for a moment he couldn't draw in any air. Smoke filled the area around them and pain reverberated through his body.

After a few seconds his military survival instincts, along with a healthy dose of adrenaline, kicked in and he rolled over and belly-crawled toward Tess, who was sprawled on the ground just a few feet away.

"Tess! Are you all right?"

She let out a low moan and lifted a hand to her head. "Hurts," she whispered.

"Stay down," he ordered, covering her body with his as much as possible. He had no way of knowing if the explosion was only a precursor to more violence or not, but he wasn't taking any chances.

Not when Tess's life was at stake.

"What happened?" she asked, her voice muffled against his chest.

"Another bomb," he said grimly.

That had been way too close. Tess could have been seriously injured by the blast. And this latest turn of events only convinced him more that she was the specific target.

**Books by Laura Scott**

Love Inspired Suspense

  *The Thanksgiving Target*
  *Secret Agent Father*
  *The Christmas Rescue*
  *Lawman-in-Charge*
  *Proof of Life*
  *Identity Crisis*
  *Twin Peril*
  *Undercover Cowboy*
  *Her Mistletoe Protector*
\*Wrongly Accused
\*Down to the Wire

\*SWAT: Top Cops

## LAURA SCOTT

grew up reading faith-based romance books by Grace Livingston Hill, but as much as she loved the stories, she longed for a bit more mystery and suspense. She is honored to write for the Love Inspired Suspense line, where a reader can find a heartwarming journey of faith amid the thrilling danger.

Laura lives with her husband of twenty-five years and has two children, a daughter and a son, who are both in college. She works as a critical-care nurse during the day at a large level-one trauma center in Milwaukee, Wisconsin, and spends her spare time writing romance.

Please visit Laura at www.facebook.com/LauraScottBooks, as she loves to hear from her readers.

# DOWN TO THE WIRE

## LAURA SCOTT

⟨H⟩ **HARLEQUIN**® LOVE INSPIRED® SUSPENSE

Recycling programs
for this product may
not exist in your area.

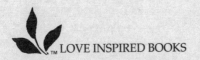

™ LOVE INSPIRED BOOKS

ISBN-13: 978-0-373-67636-1

Down to the Wire

www.Harlequin.com

**Printed in U.S.A.**

This is the message we have heard from Him
and declare to you: God is light;
in Him there is no darkness at all.
—*1 John* 1:5

This book is dedicated to my wonderful husband,
Scott, who has done everything possible
to support my writing. I love you!

# ONE

Tess Collins stood at the front of the classroom, looking out at her new group of fourth graders. More than halfway through their second week of school, things were beginning to settle down. These were her students for the next nine months. For better or worse, she thought wryly.

"Good morning, everyone," she greeted her children with a smile. "Please take your seats."

The twenty-two fourth graders radiated energy but obligingly wiggled into their assigned seats. She checked to make sure none of them were absent, before she turned back to her desk. One glance at her seating chart confirmed that a few of the little rascals had switched spots.

"Ellen and Tanya, please return to your proper seats. Hunter and Brett, I also need you to go back to your assigned seats."

The four kids gaped in surprise but giggled and shuffled around until they were seated at their correct desks. She decided not to make a big deal out of their prank, at least for now. If they continued to misbehave, she'd have to make them stay after school to have a little chat.

"Today we're going to start with a math quiz that should be a review from what you learned last year." She ignored the low moans of protest. "Miles, will you please help me hand out the papers?"

Miles, a short redheaded boy with lots of freckles, jumped up and took half of the stack of quizzes from her hands. She handed out the papers on one side, looking over the rest of the class as he passed a quiz to each student on the other side.

"Olivia, please put your book away. Only pencils and erasers are allowed." Tess waited until the young girl put her paperback away before glancing up at the clock. "Everyone ready? You may begin."

Instantly, all the students turned their attention to her impromptu math quiz. Satisfied they were all working diligently, Tess took a seat behind her desk to check out her lesson plan for the rest of the day.

*Click.*

Tess froze, the tiny hairs on the back of her neck lifting in alarm when she realized her knee had bumped into something hard. Battling a wave of trepidation, she bent sideways to see her knee was pressed up against a small box with lots of wires sticking out from it. The box was somehow attached to the inner side of her desk and there was a tiny red digital display with numbers counting down.

A bomb?

For a moment she simply stared in horror, barely believing what she was seeing. Afraid to move, fearing that releasing the trigger might cause an immediate blast, she glanced out at her students, who were all concentrating intensely on the pop quiz. Watching all those innocent faces, she grimly realized there wasn't a moment to waste.

"All right, class, we have a change in plans. Turns out we're going to have a fire drill. I need everyone to line up with their buddy and walk down the hall toward the principal's office just like we did the first day of school. I want you to go all the way outside. *Now!*"

The kids looked around in confusion but were more than happy to abandon their math quizzes. She quietly urged her students to hurry, unable to bear the thought of anything happening to them.

"Miss Collins, aren't you going to come, too?"

Trust Miles to be concerned about her. He was the sweetest child and she was often struck by the resemblance to her brother, Bobby. Although

Bobby was a sullen seventeen-year-old now, a far cry from the loving younger brother he used to be.

"Not right now. But, Miles, I want you to tell the principal to come and see me, okay? Now go outside, but walk, don't run."

Tess held her breath waiting for the students to follow her instructions, walking out of the classroom and then down the hall. She closed her eyes in relief when the last pupil was out of harm's way.

*Thank You, Lord.*

"Tess?" Evelyn Fischer, the elementary school principal, came into the classroom, a concerned frown furrowed on her brow. "What's going on?"

She swallowed hard and tried to remain calm. "Listen, you need to get every student and teacher out of the building, immediately. Tell them it's a fire drill. And then I need you to call 911, because I'm afraid I've triggered a bomb… and if this timer is correct, we only have thirty minutes until it blows."

Declan Shaw set aside his M4 .223 and pulled his ear protectors off with a disgusted sigh. "I'm still only hitting the bull's-eye at sixty-five percent."

"Hey, you're getting better," his buddy Isaac

Morrison pointed out. "The rest of your shots are in the next closest rim. That's not half-bad."

"Yeah, I think you're improving, Deck," Caleb O'Malley added. "Stop being so rough on yourself."

"We're down a sharpshooter," Declan pointed out. "Which means I need to step up my game."

"Your game is fine," Caleb assured him.

Their phones rang simultaneously, and Declan reached for his, knowing this couldn't be good news. "What's up?"

"Bomb threat at Greenland Elementary School," their new boss, Griff Vaughn, said. "Get ready to roll."

Declan didn't hesitate but ended the call and shouldered the M4 before leading the way through the training facility to the front of the building housing the sheriff's department. Isaac and Caleb were close on his heels.

"Probably a false alarm," Isaac muttered as they quickly donned their protective vests and the rest of their SWAT gear. "Some student pulling a prank to get out of school."

"Doubtful," Declan said grimly as he headed out to the armored truck. "Have you forgotten how we've had two other very real bombs within the past month, including one at the minimart that injured my sister? I don't think it's a bogus call at all."

"Most likely the same perp who seems to be targeting areas where students hang out—the custard stand, the minimart and now the elementary school. We need to catch this guy, and quick," Caleb added as he automatically slid into the driver's seat.

Declan knew that he'd be the lead point person during this tactical situation. He might not rock at being the top sharpshooter on the team, but he was the best when it came to disarming bombs.

Provided they could get there in time.

Declan tucked in his earpiece and flipped the switch on his radio. "Give me the intel," he ordered.

"We have a box with a trigger and a timer fixed underneath the fourth grade teacher's desk. She heard a click when she sat down and was smart enough to send the kids outside right away."

His gut clenched as he realized there was a possible victim close to the device. His sister, Karen, was lucky to only have suffered bruises and a broken arm, when she could easily have died from the force of the blast, just like his teammate. Once again, he couldn't help wishing he'd been the one called to the scene at the minimart. He wanted to believe his being there might have made a difference.

"Have you swept the school to make sure

everyone is out and there are no other explosive devices?"

"Affirmative. The teacher managed to get almost everyone evacuated before we arrived. We're going through the rest of the building now, but so far it looks as if there's only the one device. We won't be able to use the robot on this one."

"Keep searching the rest of the building, until it's clear. We'll be there in five," Declan assured him.

"So it's the real deal, huh?" Isaac asked.

"Sounds like it. And there's an innocent victim involved, too. So step on it, Caleb."

"Like he isn't already going pedal to the metal with lights and sirens?" Isaac muttered. "Cool your jets, man."

Declan bit back a sarcastic reply, knowing his buddy was right. He needed to get his mind in the zone if he was going to be successful at disarming the explosive device in that classroom.

He went through his pack, double-checking to make sure he had all the equipment he'd need. Two weeks ago, he'd successfully dismantled the bomb that was found behind the counter at the custard stand. He wanted to believe he'd be able to take care of this latest bomb, too. So far they'd been fortunate that they hadn't suffered more casualties. Although losing three people after the minimart blast, one cop and two civilians, was three too many.

Declan took a deep breath and let it out slowly. When they arrived, the area around the school was vacant. The first cops on the scene had done a good job of getting all the students and faculty as far away from the building as possible. Caleb pulled up to the front door and Declan was the first with boots on the ground, his pack slung over his shoulder.

"I'm going in," he told them. "Isaac, you and Caleb stay here but keep the lines of communication open. I may need some assistance."

"Roger that," Caleb said. "We'll be ready."

Declan gave a brief nod before following the cop back into the school. The hallways were lined with coat hooks that were hung at what seemed like dwarf level. Even though he'd gone to school here, the place didn't look at all familiar now that he was seeing the building through adult eyes. Then again, he hadn't set foot inside a school since barely managing to graduate from Greenland High ten years ago.

He'd signed up to join the marines and left town a couple of weeks later, without looking back. After completing his six-year commitment, including two tours in Afghanistan, he'd returned home to join the Milwaukee County

SWAT team to help support his older sister, Karen, and her young twin daughters.

"Third door on the right," the cop said, hanging back in a way that made it clear the guy didn't want to go much farther.

"Thanks." Declan nodded at him, then headed toward the classroom.

He strode through the doorway, sweeping his gaze over the empty desks, papers and pencils scattered all over the floor. He zeroed in on the slender woman seated at the teacher's desk. Her long wavy blond hair was pulled back from her face, and when she turned toward him, his gut wrenched with recognition.

"Tess?" He blinked, wondering if he'd made a mistake. But as he came closer, he knew he hadn't. Tess Collins had been a year behind him in high school, but they'd never really been friends. She was the class valedictorian, while he'd been the town troublemaker. They'd rarely spoken until the night he'd saved her from an assault mere weeks before he joined the service. He wasn't sure why she wasn't a doctor the way she'd planned, but there wasn't time to wander down memory lane.

"Don't move, okay? I'm going to take a look at this device and see what I can do to get you out of here."

"Declan," she whispered faintly. And despite

the seriousness of the situation, he was secretly pleased that she'd remembered him, too. "I thought you joined the marines."

"I did, but now I'm back." He didn't want to scare her by pointing out how precarious her situation was, so he chose his words carefully as he gave an update through his radio. "Isaac, this looks to be a homemade device, although it appears the perp stuck a lot of extra wires into it, probably hoping to cause confusion."

"Roger, Deck. Is there a timer?"

"Affirmative. We have less than twenty minutes and counting." He knelt beside her and opened his pack. "I don't want you to worry, Tess. Just stay as still as possible."

"I'm trying," she said. "I've been telling my students for years to sit still, but I had no idea just how truly difficult a task that really was until right now."

After taking out his flashlight and peering at the device, he gave Isaac and Caleb more information. "This isn't the exact same makeup as the device from the custard stand, but I still think it's the same perp. I'm betting it has basic dynamite inside, along with tacks, just like the last one."

"Tacks?" Tess echoed in horror.

"Roger that, Deck," Caleb said. "Can you disarm it?"

"Affirmative." Declan wasn't about to say

anything else that would scare Tess more than she already was. But the fact of the matter was that the placement of the bomb was ingenious. With it tucked up against the inside wall of the desk, and Tess's knee pressed against the trigger, his ability to work around the device was severely limited. Their perp was getting smarter and bolder at the same time. Not a good combination.

"I need someone to take the teacher's place," he said. "Any volunteers?"

"I'll do it," Caleb offered.

"No way," Isaac said. "You have a wife and daughter depending on you. I don't have anyone dependent on me so I'll do it."

"No," Tess spoke up. "I'm not switching places with anyone. That's a waste of time. Just figure out how to shut it down, okay?"

Declan glanced up at her. "Tess, I want you to be safe."

"I'm not trading places, end of discussion." Her brown eyes were haunted. "I trust God and I trust you, Declan. We'll get through this."

Her faith, even after all this time, was as strong as ever and only proved once again how far out of his league she was. "Negative, Isaac. She's refusing to leave. Sixteen minutes and counting."

"I trust you, Declan," Tess said again.

Humbled by her faith, he wanted more than anything not to let her down. "I'm going to move your chair as far over as possible so I can get closer to this thing, okay?" Deck stuck his flashlight in his mouth and turned over on his back, scooting under the desk. He held the wire cutters and then painstakingly followed the various wires.

Sweat beaded on his brow, rolling down the side of his face. Normally he was glacier cold when it came to disarming bombs. He didn't mind putting his life on the line to save others. In fact, he figured this weird talent he seemed to have was his calling.

But knowing that Tess would suffer—and probably die if he failed—elevated the tension to a whole new level.

He twisted several of the wires and found the bogus ones, holding his breath as he clipped them and tugged them from the clay inside the box. When he was down to four wires remaining, he wiped his brow with his forearm.

"Five minutes and counting," Isaac said in his ear.

He didn't want to think about what Tess was going through right now. She hadn't said a word as he worked, not even to ask how close he was to disarming the bomb.

"I've got four wires left. The rest were decoys," he informed Isaac. "They're all the same color, so I have no way of knowing which one is the ground, which one is attached to the timer and which one is the live wire leading to the fuse."

"You can do it, Deck," his teammate said. "Go with your gut."

Normally that was good advice. But not now. Not when Tess was the one who'd die alongside him if he failed.

He closed his eyes and cleared his mind, trying to imagine what the device looked like on the inside. With Tess's knee pressed up against the trigger, he hadn't been able to get the casing off to see for himself.

"Three minutes and counting," Isaac said.

"Dear Lord, please guide Declan," Tess whispered. "If it be Your will, give him the wisdom and strength to disarm this bomb. We ask for Your mercy and grace, Amen."

Tess's prayer caught him off guard, but then again, praying certainly couldn't hurt. He opened his eyes, and lifted the wire cutters.

"Two minutes, ten seconds and counting," Isaac told him.

Declan stared at the wires. He grabbed the one that was farthest away from the timer. If he were the one creating the bomb, he would thread it through to come out the opposite end as a confusion tactic. He clipped it with the wire cutters. The timer stopped and he breathed a sigh of relief.

"I've got it," he muttered. He clipped the next wire and relaxed when the bomb didn't blow. "Tess, I want you to slowly move your knee away from the box."

"Are you sure?" she asked, fear evident in her tone.

"I'm sure."

She moved her knee and the trigger popped back out. And then nothing. Relief flooded him. He'd done it. But the danger wasn't over quite yet.

"I'm going to ease out from under here, okay?" Declan slid out on his back, until his head was clear. He rose to his feet and then slowly pulled her chair back until her knees were free. He helped her to her feet and she clutched his arms, as if her legs weren't strong enough to hold her up.

"I need you to get out of here. I still have to get rid of this thing."

"Come with me," she begged.

"Shh, it's okay." He pulled her close for a quick, reassuring hug, before he spoke into his radio. "The teacher is clear, I'm sending her out."

"Roger, Deck. Good work."

"Go now, and I'll be out shortly, okay?" He

hated pushing her away, but he needed her to be safe.

She stumbled a bit but then managed to get out of the classroom under her own power.

After summoning Isaac inside to lend a hand, he shoved Tess's chair out of the way and peered beneath the desk. The device had been neutralized for the moment.

But until they'd safely taken it off the desk and placed it inside the cast-iron container, there was still a chance it could detonate.

Blowing him and everything around him to smithereens.

Tess shivered and rubbed her hands over her arms, chilled to the bone despite the warm September sunshine. She hadn't wanted to leave, not until she knew Declan and the rest of the SWAT team were safe. Thankfully, no one asked her to; in fact, they requested that she stay, explaining that she still needed to give a statement.

The parking area was deserted, although there were plenty of cops along the perimeter. She saw a flash of green out of the corner of her eye, and when she swung around to look, she glimpsed a man wearing a green baseball cap, brown shirt and blue jeans hurrying away. She stared for a moment, thinking he looked familiar, but then shrugged it off. No doubt, he'd been told to steer clear of the crime scene by one of the officers.

"What's taking so long?" she asked after a long thirty-five minutes had passed.

The guy in charge, who'd introduced himself as Griff Vaughn, barely spared her a glance. "They're trying to cut through your metal desk in order to remove the device. They need to get it inside the steel box for safe transport and disposal."

Logically, she understood what they needed to do, but she was still inwardly reeling from seeing Declan Shaw again. He looked different from the eighteen-year-old she remembered. Granted, he still had his dark brown hair and penetrating ice-blue eyes, but he was bigger, more muscular than before. And his face had matured, as well. Back when he was younger, he'd worn his dark hair long enough to brush his shoulders, but now it was cut military short, giving him a tough, no-nonsense look.

They'd been as completely opposite as two people could be, yet she felt oddly connected to him, just the same.

How ironic to meet him again in yet another circumstance where she needed to be rescued.

"They're coming out, boss."

"I see them. Caleb, get the woman out of here."

"Come on, ma'am," Caleb said, taking her arm.

She didn't want to leave the vicinity, but since she wasn't exactly given a choice, she allowed the tall, lean, dark-haired man to hustle her away. She glanced up at him, remembering the brief conversation between the guys, when Declan wanted someone to take her place. Caleb was the one who had just gotten remarried, and he had a young daughter. She found herself wondering what it was like for his wife to know he went into dangerous situations every day. She shivered and imagined it couldn't be easy.

"We're clear," Caleb said into his mic.

They were too far away for her to see much, but she shielded her eyes with her hand anyway, catching a glimpse of Declan and Isaac carefully carrying a large box between them as they stepped slowly across the school parking lot. They tucked the box inside the back of the armored truck and then shut the back doors.

The two men spoke for a few minutes before the sandy-haired one opened the driver's door and slid behind the wheel. Declan jogged over to where she and Caleb were waiting.

"Good job, Deck," Caleb said as he approached.

Declan brushed off the praise with a quick shrug and focused his intense gaze on her. "Tess, we need to talk."

This must be the part where she was to give her statement. She nodded and Declan took her arm, guiding her over to another sheriff's department vehicle parked in the shade of a tall maple tree that was just barely beginning to change colors in the warm autumn sun. She glanced over her shoulder, watching thankfully as the armored truck drove away with the bomb.

She slid into the backseat, feeling inexplicably nervous when Declan joined her. He turned sideways in the seat so he could face her.

"I need you to start at the beginning," Declan said as he pulled out his notebook.

Tess explained how the events transpired in the classroom before she inadvertently triggered the bomb.

"How often do you sit at your desk during the day?" he asked.

"Hardly ever," she admitted. "I tend to stand in front of the room and walk around as I'm teaching, but I do sit down for tests. And at noon, since I normally eat a bag lunch at my desk while grading papers."

He nodded, jotting down a few notes. "Do you have anyone who might be holding a grudge against you? A boyfriend? Maybe an ex-husband?"

She blushed and glanced down at her hands entwined in her lap. "No, I'm not seeing anyone and I've never been married."

"Tess, this is important," Declan persisted, his

gaze serious. "I need you to tell me anything in your personal life that might be remotely connected to this."

She didn't understand what he was getting at. "What? Why?"

Declan paused for a moment. "I believe your desk was chosen on purpose. And if you're the target, we need to figure out what connection you have to the perp."

# TWO

Tess instinctively wanted to protest, but the somber expression on Declan's face forced her to bite her tongue. She thought back over the past few months. Pathetic as it sounded, she led a boring, noneventful life. She volunteered at the church, playing piano for the choir, and couldn't imagine anyone who'd want to hurt her.

She didn't have any enemies that she was aware of. In fact, she couldn't even think of one single thing that she'd done to make anyone angry.

The thought that someone might have purposefully planted a bomb under her desk made her feel sick. She glanced at Declan, grateful to know she wasn't alone. Just like ten years ago, she felt safe with him sitting beside her.

"There isn't anyone I can think of," she said finally. "The last guy I dated was the vice principal of Greenland Middle School, but he moved last year to take a principal position down in

Missouri. I'm sure Jeff would never do something like this."

"What's his full name?" Declan asked, a frown puckered in his brow.

She sighed. "Jeff Berg. And I'm telling you, he's not involved."

"How long were you two seeing each other?"

She grimaced, wondering if this interrogation was really necessary. "A little less than four months. We weren't engaged or anything. When he told me about the job offer, I was happy for him."

"You didn't want to follow him to Missouri?"

She crossed her arms over her chest, feeling defensive. Maybe she once had a silly schoolgirl crush on the younger version of Declan, especially after he'd saved her from that disastrous prom date with Steve Gains, but at the moment, she didn't much like the man he'd become. Declan was all business, determined to get to the bottom of whatever connection he thought she had to the person who'd planted the bomb under her desk. There wasn't a speck of personalization in his tone.

In that moment, he reminded her too much of her father. The thought was enough to get her ridiculous schoolgirl emotions back under control.

"No, I didn't. Are we finished now? I need to get back to my colleagues."

"We sent everyone home…there won't be any school for the rest of the week," Declan said bluntly. "But I'd be happy to take you home."

"I don't need a ride, I have my car here." She pushed open her door and slid out of the seat, determined to get away from Declan's overwhelming presence and clear her mind.

She didn't get very far, because within seconds he'd caught up with her, lightly grasping her arm. "Tess, wait."

She stopped and glared at him over her shoulder. "For what?"

"Just give me a few minutes, okay? Which car is yours?" he asked.

"The grayish blue Honda Civic parked beneath the large maple tree," she retorted. "Why? Don't tell me you think there's a bomb planted there, too?"

"I'm going to make sure there isn't," Declan answered grimly.

*What?* Tess gaped at him in shock. She hadn't been serious when she made that remark, but it was clear that Declan really believed she was in danger. As upset as she was with him, when he let go of her arm, she missed his warmth.

Tess folded her arms over her chest, feeling vulnerable and alone as Declan crossed over to talk to Caleb. The two of them jogged across the parking lot to where she'd left her car and dropped to the ground to search underneath it.

She didn't want to think that she was the target of some crazy bomber, but it was difficult not to be afraid when Declan so clearly believed she was.

Maybe Declan was just being overly cautious. She simply couldn't imagine what she'd done to cause someone to hate her enough to plant a bomb under her desk, risking not only her life but those of her students.

There had to be some mistake.

"I can't see much," Deck muttered, flashing his light across the undercarriage of Tess's car.

"The car is too close to the ground," Caleb agreed. "I can't even get my head under there, can you?"

He shook his head. "Nope. I can't see anything obvious, but we'll need to get it up on a ramp to be sure."

"Yeah, good plan," Caleb agreed.

Declan took one last look before he reluctantly rose to his feet. No way was he going to let Tess drive the vehicle until he was certain it was safe. He caught Caleb's gaze across the hood of her car. "Maybe we should send a team to check out her house, too."

His friend lifted an eyebrow. "You really think she's the target?"

Declan nodded, unable to explain the niggling sensation that told him he was on the right track. "I do. But I can't prove it, at least not yet."

Caleb let out a low whistle. "Good luck trying to get Griff to buy your theory."

"I know." Declan understood their boss dealt with facts, not feelings. "Although it doesn't really matter if he believes me, since he'll expect us to cover all possibilities as we investigate anyway. All I have to do is come up with a plan to keep Tess safe."

"Well, good luck with that, too," Caleb said, flashing him a wry grin.

Yeah, he already knew Tess wasn't going to like his idea of forcing her to go underground, but he wasn't going to accept no for an answer. Not when her life was potentially in danger.

As he walked closer to Tess, he couldn't seem to tear his gaze away from her. Even wearing her business casual teacher's attire—gray slacks paired with a bright pink sweater—she was more beautiful now than she'd been ten years ago, decked out in her fancy prom dress. Why on earth had that Jeff dude let her go so easily? Something didn't seem right with that scenario, and he silently promised himself to double-check the guy's whereabouts for the time frame in question.

"Did you find anything?" she asked, breaking into his thoughts.

He hated seeing the fear lurking in the depths of her amber eyes. "No, but we couldn't get underneath your car to really check things out."

"So now what?" she asked wearily. "I really need to get home."

He rubbed the back of his neck, wishing there was an easier way to get her to go along with his plan. "I'm going to take you to my place for a while," he said slowly. "Just until we can verify that your car and your home haven't been tampered with."

Her eyes widened. "I don't think so," she said firmly. "My younger brother gets out of school at three o'clock, and I intend to be home when he gets there."

"Your brother?" Now he was the one who was taken by surprise. "I didn't know you had a brother."

"Bobby is ten years younger than I am, so you wouldn't remember him," she explained. "He's a senior at Greenland High School."

Deck frowned. "And he lives with you and not your parents?"

She hesitated and then nodded. "My parents died in a car crash right after my college graduation. Bobby was only eleven, so I used my science degree to become a teacher and moved into my parents' home so he wouldn't have to switch schools."

He was impressed that she took on the responsibility of raising her brother, and that also explained why she didn't follow her dream to become a doctor. There'd be time to find out more about that later, because right now he needed to stay focused.

"Okay, then you can both come to stay at my place." Declan understood Tess wasn't about to expose her brother to danger, and he didn't blame her. "At least until we know you're safe."

Tess sighed. "Look, I know you're being extra careful, and I do appreciate your concern, but I'm not at all convinced that I'm really in danger. Why is it so hard to believe this bomb was just as random as the other ones?"

"What makes you think the others were random?" Declan countered. "If my memory serves me correctly, you worked at the custard stand during high school. And I'm sure you stopped by the minimart at some point, too."

The way she dropped her gaze told him he was definitely on the right track.

"In fact, the more I think about it," he continued, "the more I'm convinced that you really are the target. And I plan to protect you while we figure out what connection you have to the mastermind behind the bombings."

Tess didn't like ultimatums, especially those given by a bossy, take-charge guy like Declan. He was crazy if he thought she was going to let him run her life.

She'd been taking care of herself and her younger brother just fine for the past six years. Jeff had tried to run her life, too, demanding she do things differently, which really meant *his way*. He'd specifically expected her to be stricter with Bobby which she refused to do. As a result, she'd broken things off with him a few weeks before he'd gotten his promotion. Jeff's moving away was a blessing in disguise as far as she was concerned.

She refused to believe she was a failure at being a parental role model. She knew first-hand what it was like growing up in a super strict household. Her father had controlled almost every aspect of her life and she'd refused to do the same thing with her brother. Granted, Bobby was going through a rebellious phase, but she didn't think his behavior was that much different than most teenagers'. Deep down, she knew her brother still loved her. Even if he didn't often show it.

"Tess?" The way Declan called her name made her realize she'd been lost in her thoughts.

"What? Oh, I'm not going home with you, Declan. I'll give you an hour to clear my car, and then I plan on picking up my brother and we'll go to a hotel if that makes you feel better."

She sensed he wanted to argue with her, but he gave a curt nod. "Fine, I'll agree with one minor change. You need to let me drive you to pick up your brother and take you both to a hotel, because I can't guarantee we'll be able to clear your car that fast."

"Deal. Where are you parked?" she asked, glancing around the area.

Her gaze fell on the man wearing the green baseball cap who was lingering near the maple tree where she'd parked her car. She narrowed her gaze, squinting against the sun. He had to be the same guy she saw earlier. And as before, she thought he seemed familiar. "Who is that guy?" she asked, talking more to herself than to Declan.

"Who?" Declan asked sharply.

"That man in the baseball cap standing near my car. I saw him earlier, too."

As if the guy in question could feel their gaze on him, he turned and disappeared behind the tree.

"Caleb!" Declan shouted, sprinting off after the guy. "Come on! We need to follow him."

"Who?" Caleb demanded as he ran after Declan.

Tess couldn't tear her gaze off the two men as they raced toward the area where the stranger had disappeared. She was so intent on watching them that she didn't notice Griff Vaughn, Declan's boss, come up beside her.

"What's going on?" he demanded with a deep scowl.

"I saw a guy over there, the same one who was here earlier," she explained. "But I don't get why Declan is so concerned about him. I'm sure he's just some curious bystander who wants to know what's going on."

"Maybe, but sometimes criminals return to the scene of the crime because they like to watch the chaos they've caused."

"I never thought of that," Tess admitted with an involuntary shiver. She was about to tell Griff about how the guy seemed familiar, when she noticed Declan and Caleb were on their way back.

Their boss jogged over to meet them and the three of them spoke for several minutes before they all turned to face her.

Declan gestured for her to come over by him

while Griff and Caleb headed over toward a large unmarked black van.

"I guess you didn't find him?" she asked as she approached Declan.

"No, but we want you to view the videotape of the scene to see if you can spot him for us," Declan explained.

"Video?" she echoed. "What kind of video?"

"Video surveillance of the crime scene, including anyone observing from the sidelines," Declan explained. "We routinely take several hours of film, just in case. We use the film from the media, too."

"Yes, your boss mentioned how criminals often return to the scene to watch." She could barely comprehend this shocking new development, but she followed Declan to the back of the van. When he opened the doors, she was surprised to see the massive amount of technology that was located back there.

"Wow," she murmured. "I had no idea you had all this stuff going on."

Declan helped her inside. "Nate is a whiz with electronics," he said. "Do you have the video ready?" he asked.

"Sure thing, Deck." Nate Jarvis, a tall, lanky blond pulled up a stool and gestured for Tess to take a seat. "We're going to start at the beginning, and I want you to let me know if you see the guy you spotted just a few minutes ago."

Tess nodded, blinking to help her eyes adjust to the darker interior of the van. She leaned close, staring at the video screen full of dozens of people standing around the perimeter of the school parking lot, and tried to catch a glimpse of either the green ball cap or the guy's brown shirt. Of course he wore colors that blended in with the crowd and the trees.

For several long minutes no one said anything, and as much as she tried to stay focused on the videotape playing in front of her, she was far too conscious of Declan crouched beside her.

*Ignore him,* she told herself, keeping her eyes glued to the video screen. They were mere acquaintances, nothing more, a fact that suited her just fine.

She was so preoccupied she almost missed the brief flash of green. "There!" she said excitedly. "That might be him."

Nate fiddled with the controls, going backward to capture the image and then moving forward in slow motion. He froze the image. "Is this the guy?" he asked.

She gnawed on her lower lip, staring at the blurry figure. "Maybe, but the way he's looking down at the ground, I can't be positive."

"I can't seem to get a good image of this guy's

face," his tech-savvy teammate muttered, going through several frames. "It's almost as if he knows we're videotaping the crowd."

"I think it's him, but maybe we should keep looking," Tess said, biting her lip.

"You're doing great," Declan murmured encouragingly. "Take your time."

She was glad he'd dropped the demanding tone. She continued watching the videotape but was disappointed when she didn't see the strange guy.

But then, just as the camera switched direction, she saw him. "There he is," she said urgently. "That's exactly when I saw him, too, as he was walking away from the area."

"Got him," Nate declared, freezing the image. "Too bad it's not his face, though. And it's hard to tell what color his hair is beneath that baseball cap."

"I know," Declan agreed.

"I'll see if I can keep working the images to make them sharper," his colleague said.

She glanced over her shoulder at Declan. "I remember thinking at the time that one of the cops must have told him to get lost," she admitted. "Do you think it's possible someone spoke to him?"

Declan shrugged. "We can ask," he murmured.

"Although I don't know if anyone would remember him."

"How about if I print off a copy of the image?" Nate offered. "It's better than nothing at the moment."

"Sounds good."

Tess stared again at the indistinguishable figure, wishing she could pinpoint what seemed so familiar about the guy. Without seeing his face, it was impossible to guess his age. Was he one of Bobby's friends? Or a neighbor? Maybe Allan Gray, the rather odd neighbor who was always overly anxious to help her?

"Let's give this printout to Griff," Declan said. "He can ask all the cops here on the scene whether anyone else recognizes him."

Tess took Declan's offered hand to step down from the van, letting go as soon as she was on solid ground. Despite the jolt of awareness that had just sparked between them, she refused to give in to the schoolgirl crush she'd once had on him. Because, just as they had been back in high school, they were still two completely different people.

She couldn't afford a relationship, even if she wanted one, which she didn't. Maybe all men weren't as controlling as Jeff and her father, but Declan certainly seemed to be. Besides, she needed to stay focused on keeping her brother out of trouble. And that was truly a full-time job.

Declan walked up to his boss and handed over the photo. The two men spoke briefly, and Griff passed Declan a set of keys, before Declan turned back toward her. "Okay, we're clear to leave."

She smiled in relief. "Good."

"It's that SUV over there," Declan said, gesturing at the police vehicle that was parked closest to her car.

"You don't have assigned cars?" she asked as they headed across the parking lot.

"Yes, we do, and that's the one I normally drive, although today Sam Irving drove it here. Caleb agreed to give Sam a lift back."

"Are you sure all this is really necessary?" Tess asked.

Before Declan could respond, a ball of fire exploded in front of them, sending her stumbling backward. She hit the ground hard, moments before everything went black.

# THREE

The force of the blast sent Declan flying backward against the pavement. The breath was knocked from his lungs and for a moment he couldn't draw in any air. Smoke filled the area around them, and pain reverberated through his body. After a few seconds his military survival instincts, along with a healthy dose of adrenaline, kicked in and he rolled over and belly crawled toward Tess, who was sprawled on the ground just a few feet away.

"Tess! Are you all right?"

She let out a low moan and lifted a hand to her head. "Hurts," she whispered.

"Stay down," he ordered, covering her body with his as much as possible. He had no way of knowing if the explosion was only a precursor to more violence or not, but he wasn't taking any chances.

Not when Tess's life was at stake.

"What happened?" she asked, her voice muffled against his chest.

"Another bomb," he said grimly, watching the SWAT members that were still on the scene disperse and cover the area, rifles held ready. He craned his neck in order to see behind him. A small fire still burned near the maple tree where Tess had seen the guy in the green ball cap.

Had that dude been the perp who'd set the bomb? Most likely, although Declan couldn't afford to ignore the possibility of the guy being nothing more than a curious onlooker, either. He'd try to keep an open mind even though the stranger was currently the best lead they had.

"I can't breathe," Tess gasped, pushing against his chest.

"Sorry." He shifted a bit so that he wasn't quite crushing her, but he wasn't willing to move away completely until he knew the area was clear.

"Deck, are you and Tess all right?" Caleb asked, coming over to kneel beside them.

"I think we're okay. Are you sure the area is secure?" He was only slightly reassured that he hadn't heard the sound of gunfire.

"So far there's no sign of anyone or any other devices," Caleb told him. "We need to get you both out of here, though. How badly are you hurt? We have an ambulance on the way."

Declan pushed himself upright but hovered protectively over Tess. "I'm fine," he assured Caleb. "Tess, where do you hurt?"

"Everywhere," she admitted with a grimace. She struggled to sit upright, and Declan eased his arm around her shoulders to offer support. The way she leaned heavily against him made him realize she might be hurt worse than he suspected.

"Take it easy," he murmured. "Did you hit your head?"

Tess put her hand to the back of her head. "Yes, I might have blacked out for a moment or two. I can feel a lump, but there doesn't seem to be any bleeding."

Declan battled back a wave of fury. That had been way too close. Tess could have been seriously injured by the blast. And this latest turn of events only convinced him more that she was the specific target.

"Come on, let's get her to safety," Caleb urged.

Declan was totally on board with that plan. He helped get Tess up and on her feet and with Caleb's assistance, walked her over to the back of the van where Nate had opened the doors for them.

"Sit down, Tess," he instructed. "Do you have

a first aid kit handy?" he asked Nate. "She could use an ice pack."

"I'm fine," she said. "I'm sure you have a few bumps and bruises, too."

He did, but that was a by-product of his job. Tess was a fourth grade schoolteacher, and he was fairly certain she wasn't accustomed to being thrown off her feet by a bomb.

Nate handed him the ice pack and he quickly twisted the bag to activate the coolant inside and gently pressed it against the back of Tess's head. Despite her earlier protest, she put her hand back there to help hold the ice pack in place.

"Just relax, I'll hold it for you," he told her.

"Did you notice that both your SUV and Tess's car were damaged by the explosion?" Caleb asked in a low tone. "The maple tree was knocked over, too."

"Yeah, I did. And I don't believe in coincidences. I need to get Tess someplace safe."

"I'm not going anywhere without my brother," she said, joining the conversation.

"I know, we'll take him with us," Declan promised.

The wailing sound of a siren indicated the local authorities and the ambulance were getting closer. He appreciated the additional backup, but at the same time, he wanted nothing more than for Tess to get the medical care she needed and then to get her out of there.

Before the bomber made yet another attempt on Tess's life.

Ignoring the pounding inside her head wasn't easy, but Tess knew that was the only way she could avoid going to the hospital. She stared down at her trembling fingers, and did her best to remain calm even though she was still reeling from being so close to the explosion.

*Dear Lord, thank You for keeping me and Declan safe from harm. And please watch over Bobby, too. Amen.*

"Tess? Is something wrong?"

Declan's concern was touching, but she knew that she couldn't keep leaning on him for support like this. They were just temporary allies. As soon as he had her safely tucked away, she knew that he'd go back to his SWAT team, leaving her and Bobby alone.

"I'm fine, but I'm anxious to see my brother."

"First we need the EMTs to check you out… you said yourself that you blacked out for a minute."

"I said I *may* have blacked out for a minute, or it could be that my brain simply shut down for a moment, from the shock of the explosion." She didn't appreciate his using her own words against her. "It's not like I find myself in harm's way like this very often."

"I know, but you could have a concussion. Give me a little more time here, okay?"

As if she had a choice. The only reason she wasn't pushing the issue right now was that Bobby was in school, surrounded by teachers and dozens of kids. He'd be fine there until she could get there to pick him up. At least she was fairly certain he'd be fine.

She winced at the shrillness of the siren as the ambulance pulled up. Within moments two EMTs had taken up residence on either side of her.

"Anyone else injured?" one of them asked.

"No, just Tess. She has a lump on the back of her head," Declan said, removing the ice pack so they could examine her.

"We were both knocked off our feet," Tess felt compelled to point out. "You should check him for injuries, too."

"I'm not hurt," Declan said firmly.

*Stubborn man,* she thought, as the EMTs poked and prodded at her. They took a set of vital signs and asked her dozens of questions to make sure her brain hadn't been knocked off-kilter. She scowled, knowing there was a very good chance that Declan had a bump on the back of his head, too.

"We should take her to Trinity Medical Center to have a CT scan of her brain, just to make sure there's no internal bleeding," the EMT on her right said.

"Okay," Declan agreed.

"No, I don't want to go to the hospital." She glared at Declan, trying to get him to drop the idea. "I'm sure I'll be fine."

"There's no need to be nervous," Declan told her. "CT scans don't hurt and we'll still have time afterward to pick up your brother."

There was that commanding tone again, and just hearing it made the hairs on the back of her neck stand up. Why did so many men like to give orders? Why did everything have to be done their way? "Have you ever been to the E.R. at Trinity?" she asked in exasperation. "Getting cleared could take hours and be a complete waste of time. I'm not going, end of discussion."

Declan wasn't happy with her decision, and neither were the two EMTs.

"You'll have to sign a release form," the guy on her left informed her. He placed a metal clipboard in her lap and handed her a pen. "Sign here," he instructed. "This means you can't come after us if you suffer a massive head bleed later."

She sensed he was trying to scare her with that comment, so she ignored it, signed her name and handed the clipboard back to him.

"Do you have another ice pack in there? This one is already getting warm," Declan said. "I'd like to try to keep the swelling down."

"Sure." The EMT took a prefilled ice pack out of his kit and gave it to him. Once again, Declan applied it to the lump on the back of her head.

She was tempted to tell him to use the ice pack on himself, but held her tongue. No sense in antagonizing Declan now, not until they'd picked up Bobby from school.

And by then, she'd be glad to see the last of Declan Shaw for a while.

"Hey, Deck, you need to come over here and see this."

Declan glanced over at Caleb and nodded. "Sure. Nate, will you keep an eye on Tess for a few minutes?"

"I don't need a babysitter," Tess muttered.

"No problem," the other man said.

Declan wished there was a way to force Tess to go to the hospital, but since she signed herself out of the EMTs' care, he didn't think there was much more he could do. Her stubbornness might have been cute if it wasn't so annoying.

He headed over to where Caleb waited. Together they canvassed the scene of the explosion. The fire had been doused by the members of his team, but the burned-out area looked awful, especially with the maple tree being uprooted by the force of the blast.

"I think the center of the explosion was in this area here," Caleb said, pointing to the blackened area. "The perp must have covered it with leaves and branches or we would have seen it."

Declan nodded thoughtfully, agreeing with Caleb's assessment. "We went right past this area to chase the guy with the green baseball cap."

"I know. It's possible he set the bomb and then took off running," Caleb mused. "But he took a chance...what if we had caught him and brought him back this way? He risked blowing himself up at that point."

"I know, but we still need to find that guy, which would be much easier to do if we had a face shot."

"Nate is going to work on enhancing the image, so maybe we'll at least be able to get a hair color as an identifier."

Declan scowled. Knowing the guy's hair color wouldn't help them much. "All right. Anything else here that might give us a clue?"

Caleb shook his head. "Not yet. We'll keep looking, but right now it's appearing to be more of a crime of opportunity than a planned attack."

"Putting the bomb under Tess's desk seems to have been a definite plan, but I'm not so sure that the custard stand or the minimart bombings were thought out the same way. Who is this creep and why does he like setting off bombs?"

"I don't know, but we'll find him." Caleb's tone radiated confidence.

Declan wished he could say the same. Oh, he knew they'd find the guy eventually, but how many other casualties would there be before that happened?

"I'm going to drive Tess over to the high school to pick up her brother," he told Caleb. "I'll be in touch later."

"Sounds good."

Declan crossed over to his boss and arranged for a different vehicle to use for a couple of hours. Griff handed over a set of keys and he took them gratefully before heading back over to Tess, happy to see she was standing up under her own power.

"Are you finally ready to go?" she asked.

"Yeah, the boss gave us his wheels to use. Right over here," he said, heading toward one of the other SUVs on the scene.

"How on earth do you tell them apart?" she asked when he opened the door for her.

"No big secret, we go by the license plate numbers." He closed the passenger door and then went around and slid into the driver's seat.

"We'll pick up your brother and get you both settled into a hotel, okay?"

"Okay." Tess seemed resigned to spending the next hour or so in his company, and if he was interested in some sort of relationship, his ego might have been bruised by her lack of enthusiasm.

But he had no intention of getting personally involved, especially not with a woman like Tess Collins. She was the type who would want a family, and that wasn't for him. His father had been an angry drunk, lashing out with his fists if Declan didn't move fast enough. He knew exactly what genes were in his DNA, and he wasn't about to tempt fate.

Besides, ten years ago, after he'd rescued her from that jerk of a prom date, all he could think of was kissing her, but instead she'd told him she'd pray for him. Really? Not that he didn't appreciate her intent, but still, what did he know about church and prayer?

Not one thing.

And he really had no interest in finding out. Caleb might have joined the church thanks to his wife Noelle's influence, but Declan wasn't about to follow along.

Tess didn't say much as he drove into the parking lot of Greenland High, but he noticed she scanned the cars as if looking for someone.

"What kind of car does Bobby drive?" he asked as he parked in the visitor lot.

"A used blue GMC truck. It's about ten years old."

Declan filed that information away for future reference. They walked up to the front entrance and stepped inside the school. Tess headed for the office and he followed, thinking about all the time he'd spent in the principal's office back when he was a student. Not some of his fonder memories, that's for sure.

"Hi, Mrs. Beckstrom, I need to see Bobby Collins," Tess said.

"There's a bit of a family emergency," he added, when Mrs. Beckstrom frowned, obviously put out at taking a student out of class in the middle of the day.

The secretary took one look at his uniform and nodded her agreement. "Of course. I'll see if I can find him."

But when the secretary returned a few minutes later, she wasn't smiling. "I'm sorry but Bobby isn't in the cafeteria. He must have left the campus for lunch. I'm afraid you'll have to wait until he returns."

"All right, what time does his next class start?" Tess asked.

"Twelve-fifteen. He has the early lunch period."

"Would you please call my cell number if he returns before we get back?" Declan asked. He took out one of his cards and handed it to her.

"All right," the secretary agreed.

"Thank you," Tess said before turning away.

They walked out of the office and headed back outside. Declan glanced at her. "Do you have any idea where Bobby spends his lunch hour?"

Tess shook her head. "Not really. I forgot that seniors were given the option of leaving the school grounds during lunch. So, as far as I know, he could be anywhere."

"What about Greenland Park?" Declan asked.

Her spine went stiff, and he mentally smacked himself. Of course Tess wouldn't want to go to Greenland Park considering that was where her idiot prom date had tried to assault her.

He was about to tell her never mind when she abruptly agreed. "All right, let's check out the park."

"Are you sure?"

"Yes. We have almost twenty minutes before Bobby is due back in class. We may as well see if we can find him on our own."

Tess walked back to the truck, and the dejected stoop of her shoulders bothered him. The events of the morning were obviously catching up to her, especially if her head was pounding the way his was. But he knew she wasn't going to be able to relax until she was reunited with her brother.

"It would be easier if I had my cell phone," Tess muttered. "But it sounded as if your boss wasn't letting anyone back inside the school yet."

"Sorry, but we'll get your personal items as soon as possible," he assured her.

Greenland Park wasn't very far from the high school, which was why the students liked to hang out there. He wound his way along the parkway, and when he saw a blue GMC truck parked along the side of the road, he gestured at it. "Is that Bobby's?"

Tess slowly shook her head. "No, his is a much older model. I don't remember the entire license plate number, but it starts with three letters *UTS*."

He nodded, knowing that it was a long shot that they'd even find Bobby here. It took almost ten minutes to circle the park and then from there, he decided to take a quick drive past the local fast food joints that were close to the high school.

"I don't see his truck anywhere," Tess said, rubbing a spot along her temple. "Where could he be?"

He glanced at his watch. "It's almost a quarter

after twelve now. Maybe we missed him. Your brother is probably already back at the high school."

"I sure hope you're right." Hearing the worry clearly evident in her tone, he frowned as he drove back toward the high school. Was there something more going on here? Was Bobby the type that might skip school, or who'd been hanging out with the wrong crowd? When the time was right, he planned to get more intel on her brother. By the time he'd parked the car, it was close to twelve twenty-five. His cell phone rang as he was about to open his door.

"Hello, is this Deputy Shaw?"

"Yes," he said, recognizing the school secretary's tone. "Do you have Bobby Collins there with you?"

"No, that's why I'm calling. Bobby never returned to his fifth-hour English class."

"I see. Will you please call me as soon as he does show up?" Declan asked, feeling Tess's concerned gaze boring into him. "Thanks."

"He's not there?" she asked, her voice rising in panic.

"No, Bobby didn't report to his English class. Tess, is it possible he skipped school?"

She stared at him. "I can't say for absolute certainty that he didn't skip on his own accord, but I don't think it's likely. Bobby knows he's on probation this semester, and he promised me he wouldn't ditch school. Believe it or not, he really wants to graduate."

He couldn't deny the sincerity of her tone. "Then where could he be?"

"I don't know," Tess whispered. "But, Declan, what if this crazy guy who's after me somehow got to Bobby first? What if he plans to use my brother as a way to get to me?"

Declan wanted to reassure Tess that it wasn't possible, but he couldn't lie to her.

Obviously anyone who wanted to hurt Tess would know she had a younger brother, one she'd raised for the past few years.

Finding Bobby just might lead them to the mastermind behind the bombings. He could only hope and pray they wouldn't be too late.

# FOUR

Tess couldn't bear to think of Bobby being in danger because of her. He was seventeen, old enough to take care of himself, but not if he trusted the wrong people.

And how could he protect himself from a bomb?

"I need to get home," she said, straightening in her seat. "Right now."

"Tess, it's not safe for you to go home," Declan pointed out. "There have been two attempts on your life already."

"But that's the first place Bobby will go," she argued. Was he really going to just sit there and tell her what to do? She opened her passenger-side door. "Listen, I'm going home with or without your help. So what will it be? Should I get out and call a taxi? Or will you take me home?"

Declan blew out a heavy breath. "I'll call the guys from the SWAT team to meet us out there. We need to make sure there aren't any more surprises."

The thought of a bomb being planted inside her home made her stomach churn. All the more reason to get home before Bobby did, she told herself. She closed her door with a swift thud. "Go ahead and call them, but hurry. We need to get there before anyone else."

She listened as Declan called his fellow SWAT officers to arrange for them to search her property. She was surprised Declan still knew her address from the night he'd rescued her all those years ago and had taken her home in his beat-up truck, not unlike the one she'd purchased for Bobby. Declan finished his call and then put the truck in Reverse so he could back out of the parking spot.

"I really wish I had my cell phone," Tess murmured. "It could be that Bobby is trying to call me right now."

"Do you want to call him from my phone?" Declan offered.

She nodded and took his smart phone, quickly dialing Bobby's number. Of course her brother didn't answer, probably because he didn't recognize the strange number. Still, she left him a message, instructing him to call her back on Declan's phone.

Discouraged, she stared at the screen, trying

to ignore the pounding headache she had, as Declan drove her home. He pulled up in front of her house and parked along the quiet, tree-lined street. When she moved to get out of the car, he caught her arm. "We have to wait for the SWAT team to clear your house first."

After everything that had happened that morning, she knew he was smart to be cautious, and tried to find comfort in the fact that she didn't see Bobby's truck in the driveway.

However, she did notice her neighbor Allan Gray coming out of his house to stand on his front porch, openly staring at Declan's police vehicle.

"Who's that guy?" Declan asked with a frown.

Before she could answer, Allan came striding toward them. "Are you okay, Tess?" he asked, peering at her through the passenger window.

This time, Declan didn't stop her when she pushed open her passenger side door. In fact, he climbed out of the vehicle, too, and came around to greet her neighbor.

"I'm fine, Allan," she said, forcing a smile. "How are you doing today?"

He bobbed his head and glanced nervously over at Declan, who still wore his work uniform. "I'm fine, Tess, but why is there a police officer with you?"

"Hi, my name is Declan Shaw." Greeting

Allan causally, he stepped forward to shake the man's hand. "I'm a friend of Tess's."

Tess wondered why Declan was using the friend routine instead of grilling Allan about where he was earlier that day. Allan Gray was a nice guy roughly about her age. As far as she knew he'd never been married, although he did have a full-time job working as a night-shift security guard for the local hospital. Today he was dressed in his usual baggy jeans and striped button-down shirt with a white T-shirt underneath. Allan was generally a nice guy, constantly offering to help Tess out, but she always felt as if she was walking a fine line around him. She wanted to be a nice friendly neighbor, but she also didn't want to give Allan the impression she was interested in anything more than a platonic friendship. She couldn't help thinking that he might not be emotionally stable, although he hadn't done anything to truly make her uncomfortable.

"Allan, have you seen my brother, Bobby, today?" she asked in an effort to distract him from the fact that Declan had driven her home.

"Yes, I saw him this morning, Tess," Allan said, always anxious to please. He bobbed his head again, a weird mannerism that tended to drive her a little crazy. "He left for school about fifteen minutes before you did."

She tried to smile, even though the fact that

Allan was clearly watching her way closer than she'd realized gave her the creeps. "But you haven't seen him since then, right?"

"No, I haven't seen him. Is there a problem, Tess?" Allan's attention was centered on her, as if Declan weren't standing right there beside her. "Do you need me to help you look for him?"

"There's no problem at all," Declan spoke up. "But thanks for your help, Allan. I'm glad you're keeping an eye on things here. Have you seen anything out of the ordinary this morning?"

Allan frowned. "What do you mean?"

"You haven't seen any strangers lurking around Tess's house, have you?" Declan asked. "Or noticed any vehicles that don't belong here?"

"Your vehicle doesn't belong here," Allan said in a blunt tone. "But other than that, no, I haven't noticed anything unusual."

"Okay, thanks. Here's my card. You can call me day or night if you detect something strange."

"I will." Allan took Declan's business card, looking a bit flustered. Tess knew Declan was trying to make a statement, basically warning Allan that he'd be nearby if anything happened. She only hoped Allan was savvy enough to understand Declan's subtle message.

Their brief conversation was interrupted by the arrival of several SWAT vehicles. The way

Allan's jaw dropped in shock when he saw them made her grimace.

"What's going on?" Allan asked anxiously.

"It's nothing, really. They just want to go through my house to make sure it's safe. Don't worry, I'm sure they won't find anything amiss."

Declan walked over to meet with the other members of his team, leaving her with Allan. She tried not to compare the two, but Declan was so much taller and broader across the shoulders than Allan, it was difficult not to notice.

Not that she was interested in Declan on a personal level. He reminded her too much of her father, who had been the city mayor for almost twenty years. With her father, everything was about control and image. Serving the public was admirable, but the way her father used to yell, often made her wonder if he'd used her as a way to let off steam from the pressures of his job.

Her mother had never stood up to him, either.

She shook off the painful memories, focusing instead on Declan and his team, who'd entered her house.

"What are they looking for?" Allan asked.

She glanced at him in surprise. "Surely you've heard about the bomb that was discovered at the elementary school? I imagine it was all over the news."

An odd expression filtered across his face, but

then he nodded. "Oh, yes, it was. Terrible, just terrible." Allan reached out to pat her arm awkwardly. "I'm glad you're okay, Tess, that was a close call."

A shiver of icy trepidation ran down her spine as she stared at her geeky neighbor. Close call? Did Allan know that her desk was the one where the bomb was planted? Declan had led her to believe that the details of the investigation would not be revealed to the press.

Had Allan been the guy she'd seen hanging around the parking lot? The man had seemed familiar but now that she was looking at Allan, she didn't think so.

It could be that Allan was just making that statement because she'd been in the school, not because he knew that the bomb had been planted beneath her desk. Yet she couldn't quite shake off the feeling of unease. Even though she knew it was highly unlikely that Allan had been involved, she was all too aware that she didn't feel safe standing out here without Declan.

"First floor is clear," Isaac said, meeting Declan in the kitchen.

"Agreed. Let's split up between the basement and the second floor," he directed.

"All right. Caleb and I will go down, leaving you and Nate to take the second level."

Declan acknowledged the plan with a curt nod and headed upstairs. He automatically went to the left, leaving Nate to check the rooms on the right. There were three bedrooms and one office upstairs, and since Tess kept everything neat and orderly, it didn't take them long to canvass the second level.

"Basement is clear!" Isaac shouted.

"Same goes for the second floor," Nate added.

"Which just leaves the grounds," Declan said. "Let's sweep the yard, just to be sure."

No one argued, and he suspected the bomb planted near the maple tree was fresh in their minds.

When Declan went out the front door, he noticed that Tess had made her way closer to the cluster of sheriff's department vehicles parked in her driveway. Was it his imagination or was she trying to get away from Allan Gray?

He kept his gaze focused on doing his job, but as soon as the team had finished checking the yard, he hurried over to Tess. "Everything is fine," he assured her.

"Good to know," she said softly. "Can I go inside now?"

Declan nodded, unwilling to say too much in front of her weird neighbor.

"See you later, Allan," Tess said, before turning away. Declan gave the guy a quick nod and then followed her inside.

"You can't stay here, Tess," he said the minute he'd shut the door behind him. "Just because we didn't find a bomb doesn't mean that you'll be safe here."

"You already said that, Declan," she responded testily. "I just want to see if there's any indication Bobby has been here since this morning, okay?"

Declan sensed he was skating on thin ice and tried to stay back, giving her plenty of room. Tess had been through a lot today, not to mention being worried about her missing brother. He knew better than to take her tense mood personally.

She disappeared upstairs and he stood in the living room, noticing how the side window gave a clear view of Allan's house.

Did the guy watch Tess on a regular basis? Did he have a pair of binoculars that he used to spy on her? Declan couldn't explain why he didn't like him. After all, Gray hadn't done anything overt, although he *had* admitted to watching Bobby and Tess leave earlier this morning.

Declan made a mental note to do a thorough background check on Allan Gray as soon as possible. Maybe he was overreacting, but it was clear to him that the guy was a bit obsessed with Tess.

But if the nosy neighbor was interested in Tess, why would he try to hurt her?

Declan didn't have an answer to that question, but that didn't mean the guy didn't have something to hide, either. He glanced at his watch, realizing Tess had been upstairs for a long time. Despite promising himself he'd give her some space, he found himself taking the stairs two at a time, to get to the second floor.

"Tess? Is everything okay?" he called.

For several long seconds there was no response, and he had taken several steps toward her bedroom when she emerged carrying a small suitcase.

"Why wouldn't everything be okay?" she asked, stopping short when she saw him standing there.

Declan felt stupid for worrying. What was wrong with him? Hadn't he already checked the house and deemed it safe at least in the short term?

"I'll take your suitcase for you," he offered.

She handed it over and then brushed past him to precede him down the stairs. "I want to leave a note on the door for Bobby, because I'm sure he'll come looking for me."

"All right." He followed her back down to the

main level, setting the suitcase beside the door while she disappeared into the kitchen to write her brother a note.

He couldn't help smiling when she chose a neon-green sheet of paper for her message, taping it to the front door where it could be easily seen from the driveway.

Isaac crossed over to meet them. "We'll be clearing both your vehicle and hers next, Deck. I'll let you know as soon as we're finished."

"Thanks." He clapped Isaac on the back and watched as the rest of his team made their way back to their vehicles. Then he turned to Tess. "All set?" he asked, taking the suitcase over to his car. He glanced over his shoulder, half expecting to see Allan Gray peering at them through his window.

"I guess," Tess murmured, in a less than enthusiastic tone. "I really hope Bobby contacts me soon."

He nodded, hoping for her sake that her brother would get in touch with her. The fact that they hadn't found anything at her house reassured him that the kid had probably skipped school on his own, rather than being a target for the bomber.

"Can I borrow your phone again?" Tess asked. "I'd like to send Bobby a text message."

"Sure." He handed over his phone, keeping his

attention on the road. "We could stop and pick you up a new phone."

"Really?" The spark of hope in her eyes made him feel like a jerk for not thinking of this option sooner. "That would be a huge relief."

"No problem."

It didn't take long to stop at her wireless carrier store and upgrade her current phone to a new one. When they exchanged phone numbers, he was relieved to have a way of getting in touch with her.

"So, where are we going?" she asked once they were settled back in his vehicle.

"There's a small hotel called the Forty Winks, not far from where I live. Their rates are very reasonable, and the place is clean." He remembered the location from a while ago when Caleb had been on the run, trying to clear his name. Caleb, Noelle and his daughter, Kaitlin, had stayed there for a night, and he figured if it was good enough for Noelle, it should be okay for Tess.

"As long as it's not too far from my house, then I'm fine," she said.

Fifteen minutes later, he pulled up in front of the hotel and shut off the engine. Tess slid out of her seat, heading inside the lobby, but he stopped her with a hand on her arm.

"Tess, I think it's best if I pay for the room."

She scowled and shook her head. "I'd rather pay my own way."

"It's not about paying your way, it's about keeping you safe," he said, unable to contain his exasperation. "Please don't argue about this. Don't you understand that I don't want anyone to know where you are?"

Her gaze clashed with his for several long seconds. "Fine," she grumbled. "But I think you're being overly cautious."

"Thank you." He pulled her suitcase out of the back and then followed her into the lobby. The woman behind the counter agreed to take cash for the room, probably because of his cop uniform, but insisted on having a credit card on file in case there was any damage.

Tess's room was on the second floor. When she used her key to open the door, he was glad the place didn't smell old and musty. "Thanks, Declan," she said, when he swung her suitcase onto the bed.

"Stay safe, Tess. I'll get in touch with you as soon as possible."

"I'll be fine," she reiterated.

He hesitated, not liking the thought of leaving her here alone. If it wasn't for the fact that his boss was waiting for him to report back, he'd take her out to lunch.

His phone rang, and he suppressed a sigh

when he saw that Griff was calling. "I'm on my way," he said in lieu of a greeting.

"You better be," his boss said in a gruff tone. "The FBI is here and they want to talk to you."

He couldn't hide his surprise. "We've been keeping them updated on the investigation, and they've admitted they don't think the bombs are related to terrorism. Have they changed their mind?"

"Not that I know of, but apparently they want to talk to you. So get back here, now."

"I'll be there in ten," Declan promised. He disconnected from the call and glanced at Tess. "I have to go, but you need to know that the FBI has been involved in this since we discovered the first bomb, and they may want to interview you."

She nodded grimly. "All right, let me know."

Declan had the insane urge to give her a reassuring hug, so he stepped back toward the door. "Remember, don't open for anyone but me."

"Or Bobby," she added.

"Call me if you need anything." He told himself to stop procrastinating and to leave already. After all, his boss and the FBI were waiting.

But leaving Tess wasn't easy, and he silently promised to return as soon as he'd fulfilled his SWAT duties.

* * *

Tess stared at the door, long after Declan had left her alone in the hotel room. Ridiculous to miss him when he'd been gone all of two minutes.

She gave herself a mental shake and quickly unpacked her small suitcase. She found a small bottle of over-the-counter painkillers and took a few, hoping that her headache would start to feel better. Then she sat on the edge of the bed, feeling as if she should be doing something to find Bobby.

But what could she do without a car? She could call for a taxi, that's what. Actually she'd rather rent a car, but that wouldn't work until she had her driver's license back. She made a mental note to make sure Declan returned her personal items from the school, before she used her brand-new smartphone to search for taxi services.

Twenty minutes later, she left her hotel room and went down to wait for the taxi to arrive. She was glad to have found her spare stash of cash back at the house, or she'd be totally dependent on Declan for everything.

"Where to?" the cabbie asked in a thick New York accent. She wondered why he'd moved to Wisconsin from New York.

"Jackson Park, it's on the corner of Elmhurst and Morrow."

The cabbie looked confused for a moment but then shrugged. "Okay, lady, it's your dime."

She clipped on her seat belt, staring through the window as they approached Jackson Park. There were batting cages there, and she knew Bobby used to go there when he was still playing for the Greenland High baseball team.

It was a long shot, but she couldn't think of where else her brother might be hanging out.

The cabbie pulled up to the entrance of the park, and she asked him to wait for her while she checked out the area. He didn't seem happy but reluctantly nodded.

She ran up to the batting cages, sweeping her gaze around the parking lot to see if she could spot Bobby's truck. There wasn't any sign of the truck or of Bobby himself, when she went from one batting cage to the next.

Discouraged, she returned to the taxi. She wasn't surprised he'd kept the meter running and she gave him the address of another park, one on the other side of the city.

But Bobby wasn't there, either. She had the cabbie swing by the school one last time, before heading back to the hotel. Eighty-five dollars later, she still hadn't found her brother.

As she used the key card to unlock her door, her new phone rang. When she glanced at the screen, her heart leaped with excitement when she recognized Bobby's number.

"Hello? Bobby?" she answered quickly.

"Tess?"

She gripped the phone tightly, as the rest of the message was garbled from a bad connection. And then the line went dead.

"No!" She quickly punched the redial button, hoping to catch her brother, but the call went straight to voice mail. She tried over and over again, but each time the call went to voice mail.

The brief connection to her brother had been severed.

And she still had no idea if Bobby was safe, or being held against his will.

She sat on the edge of the bed, staring at her phone, her eyes filling with helpless tears.

*Please, Lord, please keep Bobby safe in Your care!*

# FIVE

Declan strove for patience as FBI agents Stuart Walker and Lynette Piermont asked him a series of questions. The same questions they'd barraged him with the last time he disarmed the bomb that had been planted beneath the counter of the custard stand. His boss, Griff Vaughn, sat beside him, a stern expression on his face.

He knew he didn't have anything to feel guilty about, but he couldn't help feeling as if he were the one on trial, instead of the perp who'd set all the bombs.

"Tell us again how you disarmed the device," Agent Walker said.

Declan suppressed a sigh. "First I found and removed all the dummy wires. Then I clipped the wire that was associated with the timer. From there, I cut the wire leading to the explosive."

"How did you know which wires to clip?" Agent Walker asked.

He shrugged and spread his hands. "I don't

know what to tell you other than I seem to have a knack for defusing bombs."

"Deputy Shaw, don't you think it's odd that you always seem to know how to disarm these devices?" Agent Walker asked, leaning forward. "After all, your fellow SWAT team member James Carron lost his life when he tried to disarm the bomb at the minimart."

Declan reined in his temper with considerable effort. "That was the same explosion that put my sister in the hospital, too, remember? I don't like what you're insinuating. So what if I happen to be good at disarming bombs? It's an uncanny gift and I don't see anyone else complaining."

Griff crossed his arms over his chest and scowled at the FBI agents. "Are you accusing one of my deputies of committing a crime?" he asked.

"No, of course not," Agent Lynette Piermont said in a consoling tone. "But you have to admit, it's a little strange that Deputy Shaw always manages to disarm these devices."

"Except for the one that went off today that nearly killed him," Griff Vaughn pointed out. "Or maybe you think that was just a ruse to derail the investigation?"

Declan appreciated his boss's support, although he was annoyed to be put in a position to need it. He tried to keep his tone even and nondefensive. "We have a suspect that was identified at the crime scene and that very likely set the bomb that caused damage to my vehicle as well as to Ms. Collin's car. We have videotape of this perp being there as well, and our crime scene tech is working to identify this man. So if you're not going to help us solve this series of crimes, then maybe you should leave us alone so we can get back to work." He didn't care that his tone bordered on rudeness.

"I agree with my deputy," Griff said. "Do you have anything besides allegations to contribute to our investigation? Because, if not, this interview is over."

"Do you have any reason to suspect that these bombings are related to terrorist activities?" Agent Piermont asked.

"No, we don't," Declan said. "I believe this is the work of someone who wants to be the center of attention. Someone who is choosing his targets because they mean something personally to him. I believe this perp is from the area."

The two agents exchanged a knowing look. Because they believed him? Or because he was from the area himself? It took every ounce of willpower to keep from lashing out in anger. How dare they insinuate he might be a suspect?

"Anything else?" Griff asked. "Because I need to debrief with my team."

"That's all for now," Agent Walker said, rising slowly to his feet. "But we'll need to be kept in the loop on your investigation. I'd like a progress report by the end of the day."

Griff grunted in what could have been an agreement or something else entirely.

Declan glanced at his boss after the two federal agents left the room. "Do you honestly believe I had something to do with this?"

"Of course not," Griff said wearily. "They're just mad that you've managed to disarm so many of these devices. And they're itching to get their hands into our investigation, which they really can't if there isn't any link to Homeland Security or say a bigger target than just these few local events. Forget about the feds for now, and let's concentrate on working this case."

Declan felt a little better, although the pall of being a suspect wouldn't go away. Was this how his buddy Caleb had felt when everyone suspected him of being a murderer? Declan couldn't even begin to imagine being tossed in jail. He took a deep breath and gathered his scattered thoughts. "I have a couple of potential suspects that I'd like to follow up on, Allan Gray and Jeff Berg. Both have connections to Tess—one is a former boyfriend and the other is a neighbor who clearly has a crush on her."

"All right, anything else?"

Declan shook his head. "Not so far. We cleared her house, and according to Caleb and Isaac, her vehicle is clean, too. Her car suffered some cosmetic damage, but it still runs."

"What about your vehicle?" Griff asked.

"Not good. The engine didn't start, so Isaac and Caleb had it towed to the garage."

Griff sighed heavily and scrubbed his hands over his face. "The sheriff isn't going to like the negative impact on the budget."

Declan understood where his boss was coming from, but what could he say? They had no way of knowing that another bomb had been planted so close to the parking lot. It was just bad luck that his truck had taken the brunt of the blast.

"I'm sorry, I'll use whatever car you assign."

"Come with me to my office. I'll see what's available." Griff rose to his feet and made his way through the building to the other side of the office area. After shuffling through a stack of paperwork, Griff found the list. "Take 7918. It should be ready to roll."

"Thanks." For a moment he almost felt sorry for his boss; dealing with the massive amount of paperwork that government agencies demanded couldn't be easy. And Griff was a huge step up from their former boss who'd tried to frame Caleb for murder.

"Get me the background information on your two suspects as soon as possible," Griff added. "I'll need to include them in my report to the feds."

"Yes, sir." Declan escaped his boss's office and went to his own cubicle to log on to the computer. He decided to run a background check on Allan Gray first, and was almost disappointed that he didn't find anything more than a couple of traffic violations.

Same thing happened when he ran the background check on Jeff Berg. He scowled and drummed his fingers on the desktop. Just because they didn't have criminal backgrounds didn't mean they weren't guilty.

He performed an internet search on Allan Gray and soon discovered that Gray actually graduated from Greenland High School the same year he had. Declan sat back in his chair for a moment, surprised by the information. What were the odds?

He stared at the photo on the screen, trying to remember back to his high school years. Declan had run with a group of troublemakers, while Allan looked to be the studious, chess club type.

No matter how hard he tried, Declan couldn't remember a single interaction with Gray, good or bad. He'd have to check out the class yearbook to see what sorts of activities Allan had done back then. Maybe that would spark some memories.

After glancing at his watch, he realized it was getting close to dinnertime and he wanted to run back over to the hotel to take Tess out for something to eat. But first he had to finish his report for his boss.

Normally he took his time, but tonight he was in a hurry. Declan typed out a brief summary of the day's events and then included a brief background sketch of the two suspects. He hit the send and print buttons with a sense of satisfaction. Despite the electronic world, the bureaucrats insisted on having their reports on paper.

As he pushed away from his desk, another thought crossed his mind. Had Allan liked Tess back in high school, too? Had he asked her out? Or had she snubbed him in some way, causing him to resent her? Was that his motive for planting bombs?

Feeling grim, Declan dropped off his report on Griff's desk and left the building, realizing he might have to move Allan Gray up to the top of his suspect list.

And he intended to ask Tess about her relationship with him as soon as possible, to see if there was any way to back up his latest theory.

* * *

Tess was relieved when Isaac called to let her know that her car had been cleared. She'd already spent a small fortune on taxicabs going to all the places she could think that Bobby might be. Back at the hotel, she called a taxi one last time, having agreed to meet Isaac at the elementary school parking lot.

Isaac was waiting near her car when she arrived, looking a little out of place with her purse tucked under his arm. He smiled when he saw her. "Hi, Tess. I have your things and we've released your car."

"Thanks," she murmured, feeling self-conscious as she took her purse from the sandy-haired deputy's hand. "Will you drive me over to pick it up? I've been going crazy without having my own vehicle."

Isaac frowned. "I know Deck wants you to stay safe, so don't do anything foolish, okay?"

"Don't worry, I intend to stay out of danger," Tess assured him. Of course, she also intended to find her brother, too, but decided not to mention that part.

Her car had lots of dents and scratches, but right now that was the least of her worries. She slid behind the wheel and started the car, heading out to the street. Where could Bobby be? She hadn't found him at any of his usual hangouts, which only made her think that it was highly likely that someone had taken him against his will.

What if they'd drugged him? Or hurt him in some way?

She took several deep breaths, knowing it didn't help to think the worst. She needed to remain calm and rational if she was going to find him.

The ride back to the hotel wasn't nearly long enough to clear her mind, and she leaned back in her car rather than heading back inside to stare at the four walls of her hotel room.

Where else could Bobby be?

Abruptly she sat up. What if he was hanging out at one of his buddies' houses? But if that was the case, why would he ignore her calls? Because he thought she'd be upset with him for skipping school? Right now all that really mattered was knowing he was all right. They would deal with the rest later.

Mentally she went through the short list of his close friends. Finn McCain and Mitchell Turner were the only two whose last names she remembered.

For a moment she dropped her forehead to the edge of the steering wheel. What sort of mother figure was she that she couldn't remember the last names of her brother's friends?

Maybe she hadn't done the best job in raising her brother, but she refused to fail him now.

Pulling herself together, she put her car in gear and headed over to Finn McCain's house. Finn lived very close to the high school, and as she drew closer, she eagerly scanned the area for Bobby's truck.

But it was nowhere in sight.

With grim determination she parked in the driveway and walked up to the front door. There were raised voices inside, male and female, causing her to pause with her hand raised to knock, remembering what it had been like when her father had yelled at her for getting a *B* instead of an *A*.

She swallowed hard and pushed the painful memories away. She rapped sharply on the door. When there was no response she leaned on the doorbell, and that worked because the loud voices abruptly stopped.

After several lengthy moments, the door opened and a big burly man with a huge belly scowled at her from behind the screen. "We're not buying whatever you're selling," he said harshly.

"Mr. McCain, I'm looking for my brother,

Bobby Collins. He's a friend of your son. Are Finn and Bobby here?"

"No." Without another word, the large man shut the door in her face.

She raised her hand to knock on the door again but then let out a sigh, knowing it was useless. Even if Bobby was here, she doubted Mr. McCain would open the door long enough to admit it.

Since she didn't see any sign of Bobby's truck, she turned around and headed back to her car.

Her head throbbed from a mixture of pain, anxiety and hunger, but she wasn't going to stop for something to eat when she didn't even know for sure if her brother was safe.

She slid behind the wheel and swallowed hard. Mitchell Turner lived in the poor side of town, in the same neighborhood where Declan had grown up. She wasn't thrilled about going over there, but at least it was still light out. And based on her reception here at Finn's house, she didn't expect her next visit would take too long.

The houses lining the streets gradually became more dilapidated and grungy the closer she came to Mitchell Turner's address. After crossing an intersection, she spotted a large group of kids lounging in the doorway of a neighborhood liquor store, and she felt her heart drop, hoping that Bobby wasn't among them. She slowed down, peering at them intently in an effort to make sure that Bobby wasn't part of that crowd.

A few of the boys stared boldly back at her and she quickly averted her gaze, tightening her hands on the wheel. A quick glance confirmed that her automatic locks were engaged, just in case.

Broad daylight, she reminded herself. Nothing to be worried about.

She caught sight of Mitchell's house, complete with boarded-up windows and several rusty car parts scattered all over the front yard, which consisted mostly of weeds. Her attention was diverted when she heard a loud crash a moment before her windshield shattered into thousands of tiny pieces.

Wrestling with the steering wheel, she tried to stay on the street she couldn't see, but despite her best efforts, the car slammed into something hard, bringing her to a teeth-rattling stop. The engine hissed and groaned and she knew she wasn't going to be able to drive even if she could see through the spider-cracked glass, which she couldn't.

Fear skittered down her spine as she numbly realized what had just happened. Someone had thrown something at her car on purpose. She slowly unclenched her fingers, remembering the group of boys she'd noticed. Had one of them caused the crash? The force of the impact had caused her purse to tumble to the floor, so she removed her seat belt and leaned over, to search for her cell phone.

With shaking fingers, she quickly scrolled through the contact list to find Declan. She called his number, hoping and praying he'd answer.

# SIX

Declan had just pulled into a fast food drive-through lane when his phone rang. He smiled when he realized Tess was calling. "Hi, Tess," he greeted her.

"There's been an—accident," she said in a wobbly voice. "I need you to come pick me up right away."

He frowned and yanked the steering wheel to the right so he could get out of the line of cars waiting for food. "Are you all right? Where are you?"

"I'm in your old neighborhood near Sixth and Forrest. Please hurry, Declan. I'm scared."

He battled back a flash of fear. "I'll be there as soon as possible," he promised. He flipped on the red lights and sirens in the vehicle so that everyone would move out of his way. He could tell by the quiver in Tess's voice that she was frightened, either because she was injured by the crash or because of the fact that she was a woman alone in the worst part of town.

Or both.

He made it to his old stomping grounds in record time, which was amazing since it was the height of rush hour. He saw Tess's car smashed up against a light post and his heart rattled in his chest as he pulled up alongside it. Through the driver's-side window, he could see Tess huddled in her seat, holding a can of hair spray.

The old neighborhood hadn't improved any over the years. He couldn't imagine what on earth Tess was doing here, but he climbed out of his car and rushed over to her. "Tess? Are you all right?"

Frank relief was mirrored in her eyes as she slowly nodded. "The door won't open," she said.

The front bumper was crushed up into the driver's-side door, so he jogged around to the other side. A good yank opened the passenger door. "Can you crawl over here?" he asked.

"Yes." She tossed the can of hair spray onto the floor of the passenger side and gingerly climbed over the console between the seats. He helped her out of the car and she clutched at his shoulders, sagging against him. "Thank you," she whispered.

He wrapped his arms around her, holding her close. He was grateful she wasn't hurt, but he didn't understand why she was here in the first place. Hadn't he asked her to stay at the hotel in order to be safe? Why on earth couldn't she have just listened to him?

"I think someone threw something at the windshield," Tess murmured, loosening her grip on his shirt. "When it shattered into millions of tiny cracks, I couldn't see."

"Did you see anyone suspicious before that?" he asked, raking his gaze around the area.

"There was a group of kids back there by the liquor store," she said in a low tone. "But they're gone now."

"We'll have to call a tow truck," he said, trying to keep his tone even. "Why don't you wait for me in my car?"

Tess shook her head, and then bent down to gather up the stuff that must have fallen out of her purse, including the can of hair spray. "I just need a few minutes to go over to Mitchell Tanner's house. He lives just a couple of houses down on the other side of the street."

Declan gritted his teeth in frustration. "Tess, you shouldn't even be out here at all!" he said, the words coming out sharper than he intended. "I thought I asked you to stay and wait for me at the hotel."

She acted as if she hadn't heard him, but before he realized what she intended, she'd looped her purse strap over her shoulder and strode down the street rather than getting into his car.

"Tess, wait!" He quickly caught up to her. "What are you doing?"

She spun around to face him, her eyes full of wounded reproach. "My brother is missing and I intend to go to his friend Mitchell's house to see if he's there."

"Tess…"

"Don't even go there," she warned. "If your sister was missing you'd be out looking for her, too."

She had a point, even though his being in danger was part of his job. He swallowed his anger and tried to keep his tone even. "Okay, fine, we'll both go."

"Suit yourself," she said with a shrug, before turning away.

Declan kept a keen eye out for any other troublemakers as they approached a run-down house. He didn't see any sign of Bobby's truck, but he knew that wouldn't stop Tess from making sure her brother wasn't here.

She didn't look at all nervous as she rapped loudly on the door. He lingered a little behind her and to the right, in case the situation went south.

There was no answer, so she knocked again, harder. After a long minute, the door opened and a woman stood there, smoldering cigarette in one hand and a glass full of amber liquid in the other. "Yeah? Wadda ya want?"

"My name is Tess Collins and I'm looking for my brother, Bobby. Have he and Mitchell been here?"

"I dunno." Mitchell's mother swayed in the doorway, and from the glazed look in her eyes, Declan knew she was intoxicated. "I don't think so."

"Please, Ms. Turner, this is important. I haven't seen Bobby all day and I'm very worried about him."

The woman tossed back the rest of her drink and then swiped her hand across her mouth. "If I see 'im, I'll have him call ya." She moved back and shut the door.

Tess's shoulders slumped as if the weight of the world rested upon them. Declan's earlier ire vanished and he put his arm around her shoulders. "Come on, Tess, I doubt Bobby and Mitchell are hanging around here."

She didn't protest as he guided her back down to the street and over toward his car. At the curb, they had to stop and wait for a car to pass by. He glanced at the driver, and then did a double take as he realized the man behind the wheel looked like Allan Gray.

"What is he doing here?" he asked, staring after the nondescript beige car. He quickly memorized the tag number, in case he'd made a mistake.

But he didn't think so. The driver had absolutely looked like Tess's neighbor. And if he didn't know better, he'd think the guy was following her.

Had he been the one to throw the rock at her windshield, too? Although, if that were the case, Gray had plenty of time to pretend to be the hero, coming to her rescue.

"This way," Declan said, turning Tess in the direction of his car. It didn't seem like the right time to mention how he thought he'd seen Gray. First he needed to run the license plate number in order to be sure.

"I have to find my brother," she whispered as he opened the car door for her.

"I know." There was no point in arguing, because he realized that Tess cared more about finding her brother than she did about her own safety.

And while he couldn't blame her, he still didn't approve of her decision to drive to the seediest part of town to look for Bobby, especially when she could just as easily have asked him to go with her. Or to have asked him to do the task himself.

Unless there was some reason she didn't want

him around when she finally caught up to her brother. The thought pulled him up short. Was that it? Was there more to Bobby's disappearance than she was letting on?

And if so, what?

Tess kept her gaze averted from Declan so he wouldn't see how close she was to losing it. First she'd been in a car crash caused by vandalism and then he'd yelled at her, just as her father used to do. And now she was no closer to finding her brother than she had been earlier that morning.

She'd been so certain that she'd find Bobby at one of his friends' houses, but instead she discovered that Bobby's friends were in horrible home situations, worse than she ever could have imagined. Even worse than what she'd endured with her father.

How was it that Bobby identified so well with these two boys? Did he really think living with her was as bad as what these boys had to deal with? Maybe she wasn't perfect, but she wasn't that bad, either. She simply couldn't comprehend what was going on with her brother.

Despair overwhelmed her. She had no idea where to look for Bobby next. And having Declan go from holding her close to basically yelling at her was too much to handle.

She sniffed, trying to fight back her tears. There had to be something she could do. But what?

Pray. She dropped her chin to her chest and squeezed her eyes shut, blocking everything else out.

*Dear Lord, if it be Thy will, please guide me in searching for Bobby. Please watch over him and keep him safe. Please grant me the patience and strength I'll need to get through these next few days, Amen.*

A sense of peace crept over her and she took a deep breath and let it out slowly, knowing that God would carry her burdens if she simply asked Him.

Tess subtly swiped away the evidence of her tears and glanced over at Declan. Now that she'd had a chance to calm down a bit, she understood that he'd been upset with her for leaving mostly because he was worried about her. She probably needed to explain about her past, but she was too exhausted to broach the subject now.

She pulled herself together, knowing that this situation wasn't Declan's fault. Furthermore, she was truly grateful for the way he'd come the moment she called.

"I'm sorry," Declan said, reaching over to take her hand in his.

Surprised, she glanced up at him. "For what?"

"I shouldn't have gotten upset with you. It's just that this place…" He paused and then shook his head. "You know this neighborhood isn't a safe place to be, even during the day. Especially not for a woman like you."

"I've been here before. I dropped Bobby off here a while ago."

Declan actually winced. "Don't tell me stuff like that. I can't stand the thought of you being anywhere near here."

She realized he was embarrassed that he'd grown up in the neighborhood. "Was joining the marines worth it?" she asked softly.

"Yes," Declan responded without a moment's hesitation. "As hard as it was to become a marine and to fight in Afghanistan, I don't regret getting the chance to leave this all behind."

She nodded, understanding without being told that Declan's life experiences must have been all too similar to what they'd just witnessed with Mitchell's mother. And she found it amazing that Declan had turned his life around, to become a member of the SWAT team, no less.

Obviously being forced to give and obey orders helped mold him into the man he was today. So she had no business complaining. Besides, she didn't care if he yelled at her, as long as they found her brother.

She closed her eyes and prayed again for

Bobby's safe return. Feeling a little more optimistic after her prayer, she sank back in her seat and stared again at her phone. If only Bobby would call or text her again.

"Let's stop for dinner," Declan suggested. "We need to refuel, and besides, if we're going to find your brother, we need some sort of plan."

"Really?" She glanced at him, afraid to hope. "You'll help me find him?"

A wounded expression flitted across his face before he nodded. "Of course I'll help you. Why wouldn't I? The only reason I left you alone in the first place was that I had to report in to work to talk to the feds."

"I know, but I thought you were mad at me." She couldn't explain how she was used to being controlled by anger and fear. *If you do exactly as I say, I'll let you stay overnight at your girlfriend's house. But if you disappoint me, you'll be grounded for a month.*

She shook off the memories, reminding herself that her father had been gone for over six years. She missed her mother, even though her mom had been kept under her father's thumb as much as Tess had been, if not worse.

"I'm not mad at you, frustrated maybe," Declan said, pulling into a well-known diner. "All I wanted was for you to wait for me so I could keep you safe."

"Yes, well, sitting in that hotel was driving me crazy," she admitted. "I needed to do something to find Bobby. But I checked everywhere I could think of without any luck."

"Where did you go?" Declan asked as he climbed out of the vehicle.

"The batting cages, a couple of other parks. And then the houses of his two best friends. Mitchell's house was my last resort." Tess tried to keep the depths of her despair from her tone.

"Come on, let's get something to eat."

She followed Declan inside the restaurant, and soon they were seated across from each other in a booth off to the side. She didn't think she was hungry, but the scent of food made her stomach growl.

"Everything looks so good," she murmured, looking through the glossy menu.

A few minutes later, a server came to give them water and to take their order. Tess treated herself to a thick juicy burger while Declan ordered the pot roast.

As soon as they were alone again, he leaned forward, pinning her with his crystal-blue gaze. "There have to be other places where your brother could be," he said in a low tone. "He must have other friends, besides the two we've already checked out."

"He doesn't talk to me about his friends," she

admitted, toying with her straw. "He always seems so alone."

"What activities is he involved in at school?" Declan pressed.

"He was dropped from the baseball team when his GPA dropped to less than 2.0," she said. "Most of his baseball buddies stopped hanging around with him after that."

"Tough break. I can see why he might be falling in with these other guys."

"Really? Because I don't get it at all," Tess said, tossing down her straw with a disgusted sigh. "Those boys come from rough backgrounds, and I just don't understand why Bobby would think that living with me is so terrible."

"Tess, it's probably not about you at all," Declan said, reaching across the table and taking her hand. "He must feel abandoned by his other friends, so he's picked the few guys who accept him for what he is."

She understood what Declan was saying, but inside she still rejected the concept. "Bobby struggles with school and I tried to tutor him myself, but that didn't work. So I hired someone else to do it, but he refused to go. If he had stuck it out with the tutor, he might not have been dropped from the team."

Declan gently squeezed her hand. "You can't go back and change the past," he pointed out.

"Right now we need to find Bobby and keep you both safe. Are you sure there isn't anyplace else he would go? A girlfriend that you might not know about? Some other place he likes to hang out, maybe to be by himself?"

She shook her head and shrugged. "I'd be the last to know about a girlfriend." The thought only depressed her more, so she shoved it away. "I checked all the places I could think of. I'm out of ideas for the moment."

Declan held her hand, his comforting touch filling her with solace until the server arrived with their food. As hungry as she was before, she found that her appetite had suddenly vanished. The few bites of her burger sat like a lump in her stomach.

"You need to keep up your strength, Tess," Declan reminded her.

"I know." She nibbled on a French fry in an effort to get something solid in her stomach. But as soon as Declan was finished eating, she pushed her half-eaten food away. "I'm ready to go," she announced.

She was impressed that he didn't harp on her again about eating. He paid the bill and she followed him out of the diner back outside.

"There used to be an old arcade in the old neighborhood," Declan said as he slid behind the wheel. "Maybe we should check that out before we go back to the hotel."

"Sure," she agreed, feeling a slight flare of hope. "Bobby loves video games."

"What kid doesn't?" Declan asked drily.

He didn't say much as they drove back to the neighborhood, and even with Declan beside her, she couldn't deny feeling nervous at the blatant looks thrown their way as they walked through the arcade.

She blew out her breath when she realized Bobby wasn't there.

"Maybe he's at the hotel waiting for you," Declan suggested after they left.

"I wish he'd call me again," she said.

Declan's eyebrows shot up in surprise. "You mean he already called you once?"

"Yes." She quickly explained that all she could hear was Bobby saying her name, before the call had been cut off.

"If he called once, I'm sure he'll call again," Declan said confidently.

She wished she could be so sure.

As Declan pulled up in front of her hotel, she turned in her seat to face him. "Thanks again, for everything."

"I'll walk you up," he said.

Since arguing would be a waste of breath, she slung her purse over her shoulder and took the steps up to the second floor where her room was located.

She pulled out her room key intending to unlock the door, but before she could slide it into the slot, she realized the door was already ajar.

"Get back," Declan said, putting out his arm to prevent her from going inside.

"I'm sure I closed it behind me," she said.

Declan held his Glock ready as he kicked the door until it was wide-open. He stayed along the edge of the wall, checking the small bathroom area first, before going farther into the room.

Tess hovered in the doorway. Even from there she could see that someone had been inside her room. Her small suitcase was lying empty on the floor and the few items she'd packed, clothes and toiletries, had been scattered carelessly around.

For a moment she could only stare at the mess in horror. Who would have done such a thing? And why?

She had no idea, but it was clear she wasn't safe here.

And the way things had gone so far today, she was beginning to believe she wouldn't be safe anywhere.

# SEVEN

Declan scowled as he went through Tess's small hotel room making sure the perp wasn't still around, hiding. He was glad Tess hadn't been here when this happened, but he didn't like the fact that someone had obviously followed her here, either.

Once he'd cleared the room, double-checking everything, he glanced back at Tess and gestured for her to come inside. "Let's gather your stuff together. We need to get out of here."

Thankfully she didn't argue and between the two of them the task didn't take long. But even when she had the suitcase packed, he went over to the doorway and stood, scanning the parking lot for any sign of danger.

Was the person who'd ransacked her room still hanging out somewhere nearby?

He couldn't afford to discount the possibility.

There were several cars in the parking lot, and he took his time inspecting them, making sure each one was empty. Or at least appeared to be empty. From his perch on the second floor, he could see into the front row of cars that happened to be parked nearby. But there were still a half dozen vehicles he couldn't eliminate as potential threats.

"Stay behind me," he said in a low tone. "We're going to take the east set of stairs down to the ground level. You'll have to carry the suitcase so that I can hold my gun just in case."

"I understand," she murmured. "The suitcase isn't heavy."

He let out his breath and made his move. The sun had disappeared behind the trees, giving them a hint of dusk as protection. Full darkness would have been better, but he wasn't about to wait around any longer.

Keeping close to the wall of the building, he led the way down the east stairway. As soon as they were on the ground level, he breathed a little easier.

"Stay down as much as possible," he instructed as he eased along the sidewalk in front of the building, using the parked cars as protection. He was glad he'd parked in the front row, and as soon as they'd reached the vehicle, he opened the passenger-side door for Tess and urged her inside.

He tossed the suitcase in the backseat and then

jogged to the driver's side. Once he was behind the wheel, he jammed the key in the ignition, cranked the engine and backed out of the parking space, mentally braced for the sound of gunfire.

But there was nothing but silence as he headed for the street. Still, he didn't fully relax until he'd driven a winding path through the subdivision, making sure they weren't followed, before he headed for the highway.

"Where are we going?" Tess asked.

Good question. He glanced over at her, wishing she'd just come and stay with him, but knowing she wasn't about to change her mind. "Another hotel, only this time, we're not telling anyone where you're staying."

Tess grimaced but nodded. "All right. But I didn't tell anyone where I was staying, either."

"Any idea what the intruder was looking for back there?" he asked.

"I have no idea. From what I could tell, there wasn't anything missing. I had my purse with me, so they didn't get any cash or my credit cards."

"You didn't put the name of the hotel on your neon-green flyer you taped on the front door of your house, did you?"

"No, the sign simply asked Bobby to call me as soon as possible."

He was glad she hadn't been more specific. First he had to rescue her from his old neighborhood and now this. As if they hadn't had enough danger so far today? A wave of frustration hit hard.

"I don't get it, why would anyone take the risk of breaking in?" Declan tried to make sense of the series of events. "If they were trying to get you, they would have been better off staking out the place and waiting for you to be in there alone."

So much for his attempt to keep her safe.

"I don't get it, either," she admitted.

"What about earlier today? Did you notice anyone following you?"

She shook her head. "I had the taxi driver take me all over the city, and I didn't notice anything unusual."

Declan drummed his fingers on the steering wheel, thinking back to that beige car he'd noticed in the old neighborhood. "I'm pretty sure I saw your neighbor Allan Gray after we left Mitchell's house. Could be that he followed you earlier. Otherwise how would he have known you'd be there?"

"Allan?" Tess echoed with a frown. "I didn't see him."

The more he thought about it, the more he figured that her neighbor had to be the key. But he shouldn't have said anything until he'd gotten proof of his license plate, like he'd originally planned. "Do you know what kind of car he drives?"

"I'm not sure, some sort of sedan, I think," she said in a doubtful tone. "But I can't be positive. I guess I don't make it a habit of spying on my neighbors." He knew what each of his neighbors drove, but being aware of those sorts of details was part of his job. Normal civilians like Tess didn't live that way. He reminded himself to look up Allan Gray's vehicle later. "Gray went to Greenland High School, too, and apparently he was in my graduating class. Did you know him back then?"

"Yes, I knew him in high school, although not very well. I think he might have been in my physics class, though."

Declan was surprised to hear they shared a class together. "Did he ever ask you out?"

"No, why would he?" She let out an exasperated sigh. "It's not as if I was a popular kid back then. I studied all the time because my father wouldn't accept anything less than straight *A's*. I spent way more time in the library than I did anywhere else. In fact, that was part of the reason I was so surprised that Steve asked me to prom. Little did I know how he planned to end the evening."

Declan frowned, remembering that night he'd stumbled upon Steve Gains attempting to force Tess into having sex with him. He was very glad he'd gotten there in time to prevent anything from happening, although truthfully, Tess had managed to save herself without a whole lot of help from him. The memory of the way she'd kicked Gains and then taken off running brought a reluctant smile.

But he was more interested in what Allan Gray was doing back in high school. "I don't remember Gray at all," he confessed. "I meant to stop at home to find my yearbook to see if anything might jog my memory. Do you know what he was involved in back then?"

"I'm pretty sure he was involved in the drama club," Tess said slowly. "I vaguely remember he asked me to join, too, so that we could be stage-hands together. At the time I thought it might be fun, but my father put an end to that idea pretty quick."

This was the second time she'd mentioned her father, and Declan was beginning to realize that Tess hadn't achieved the status of being class valedictorian because it was something she wanted to do, but because her father expected it. "Did your father want you to be a doctor?"

Her lips thinned and she shook her head. "No,

that was my dream. He wanted me to be a lawyer so that I could go into politics like he did."

"That's right, I remember now. Your dad was
the town mayor, wasn't he?"

"Yes." The pinched expression on her face
gave him the impression that these were not
happy childhood memories. And since she'd
been through enough, he decided to steer the
conversation back to the situation at hand.

"So you knew Allan back in high school,
which makes sense. But how is it that he ended
up living next door to you?"

Tess was silent for a moment. "I don't know
the exact details. But I do recall there used to
be an elderly couple who lived next door, and
they put their house up for sale after they decided to move into an assisted-living facility.
I'm sure the price was reasonable, and I guess
Allan figured it would be a good investment.
I know for a fact that he's only lived there for
about two years."

"Hmm, interesting." He wondered how much
of Allan's decision to buy the place was related
to the fact that Tess lived next door. Was it possible Gray harbored a secret obsession for Tess
that had spanned ten years?

If so, Declan could only imagine what Allan
Gray was capable of doing if he discovered Tess
didn't return his feelings.

\* \* \*

Tess rubbed her temple, trying to massage her headache away. She didn't want to think about Allan Gray or the fact that her neighbor might have been near the scene of her earlier accident.

She stared down at her phone, willing Bobby to call.

"We'll stay at that hotel up ahead, if that's okay with you."

"Sure, why not?" She glanced up and noticed that the hotel wasn't all that far from where her church was located. "Wait, pull in here," she said quickly.

"What? Why?" Declan asked, but he did as she asked and made a sharp right turn into the church parking lot.

"I need to go inside for a moment," she said, opening her door.

"Hang on a minute," Declan protested, lightly grasping her arm. "Are there services tonight? Is there some religious holiday that I don't know about?"

"No, I just need a few minutes of peace and quiet, that's all." She didn't want to explain the urge to go inside the church that she'd gone to for solace after a particularly difficult argument with her father. "Please let me go inside. I promise I won't be long."

"If you're going, then I'm going with you."

Declan's expression was pulled into a tight frown, as if he didn't appreciate her request for a little side visit, but while she felt bad, the need to go inside outweighed her guilt.

She tugged on the door, glad to find that the church wasn't locked. Pastor Tom normally locked the place down overnight, but since the hour was only seven-thirty in the evening, the doors were still open. She headed down toward the front of the church and slid into the fourth pew on the right, where she normally sat during services.

Closing her eyes, she prayed for strength and support, followed by the Lord's Prayer. When she finished, she was conscious of Declan standing in the back of the church and couldn't help wishing he'd join her in prayer.

But he wasn't a Christian, at least as far as she knew. Was that part of the reason that God had brought Declan back into her life? Not only to keep her safe, but so that she could show him the way to being a Christian?

The more the idea rolled around in her mind, the more she believed that had to be part of God's plan. After ten minutes or so, she opened her eyes and gazed up at the empty altar, feeling a little better. Being in church was so soothing she wished she could spend the night here.

Not that Pastor Tom would approve. And

besides, she couldn't ignore the fact that danger seemed to follow her wherever she went. The last thing she wanted to do was to put Pastor Tom in harm's way. The hotel that was just a couple blocks away was probably a better choice.

She was about to leave when she had an idea. Why not leave Bobby a note here? Bobby knew how much she enjoyed attending this church and that she always came early enough to sit in this pew. And he'd come on occasion, too. Maybe he'd return as a way to connect with her? Without giving herself a chance to second-guess her decision, she quickly pulled a small piece of paper and a pen from her purse, holding it in her lap so that Declan couldn't see what she was doing. Somehow she sensed he wouldn't approve.

She kept the note short. *Staying at the American Lodge. Come and find me. Tess.*

There was a crack along the edge of the pew and she quickly stuffed the note inside.

She frowned, staring at the note. Hopefully Bobby would come here seeking peace, the way he had in the past. After all, he got along pretty well with Pastor Tom. But what if he didn't? Or couldn't come?

Leaving the note was better than doing nothing and provided at least a glimmer of hope. With a sense of renewed determination, she slid out of the pew and then walked back down to where Declan waited. She caught his gaze, wondering if he'd noticed that she left the note.

Since he didn't say anything as they made their way back out to his car, she figured her secret was safe.

*Dear Lord, keep Bobby safe in Your care and please guide him to the note I've left for him. Amen.*

Declan had felt out of place even just standing at the back of the church, but since Tess was smiling, he figured the slight detour had been well worth it.

"Thanks," she murmured.

He flashed a reassuring grin. "You're welcome. Did it help?"

"Praying always manages to put things in perspective," she replied as he drove the couple of blocks to the hotel. "And I needed those few moments of prayer more than I can say. Your patience really means a lot to me."

"No problem," Declan said, feeling a bit uncomfortable with her gratitude. Obviously she didn't realize how close he'd been to refusing her request. "After the day you've had, you deserve a little peace and quiet."

"Do you attend church at all?" she asked as he pulled into the hotel parking lot.

He tried not to grimace. "Not really."

"I'd think in your line of work you'd pray a lot," she murmured. "Especially since your job places you in dangerous situations."

He wasn't sure what to say to that. He remembered listening to her prayer as he was defusing the bomb. At the time he'd been grateful for the assistance, from whatever the source. "I tried a few prayer services while I was deployed overseas," he confided. "But then after my buddy was killed, I never went back."

She glanced at him in sympathy. "I'm sorry to hear about your friend's death. I'm sure that must have been difficult."

"Yeah." Talk about a massive understatement. He'd been standing right next to Tony when he was shot. It was a quirk of chance that Declan was here today, while his buddy wasn't.

"After my parents died, I leaned on my faith a lot," she continued. "God is always there for us when we need Him."

He didn't think she'd appreciate hearing how he had returned home after losing Tony to drown his sorrows in a bottle of booze. He might still be drunk if not for the fact that Karen had needed his help to get away from her abusive ex-husband.

He hadn't touched a drop of alcohol in the four years since then, but he was keenly aware that it might not take much to send him tumbling down into that black hole. He was, after all, his father's son. And wasn't there something about how alcohol abuse tended to run in families?

Depressing thought. He refused to be anything like his father, no matter what. Just knowing they shared the same genes was terrifying enough.

"Thanks for offering to pray for me that night I drove you home after your prom date," he said.

"I prayed for you a lot," she said. "I was tempted to write to you but wasn't sure how to find your address."

That surprised him. "Really?"

"Really. I guess I should have asked around to see if anyone else knew how to reach you."

He didn't want to tell her that he was one of the few marines who hardly got any mail. Karen had written to him a few times, but then those letters had dropped off, too.

Humbling to think that Tess cared enough to at least consider writing to him. Not that she probably would have written the entire time he was gone.

Even one letter would have been great to have.

Okay, enough already. What was the point of wishing things had been different? Tess was far too good for him and a Christian, too. She deserved more than he could ever give her.

And it was annoying that he even considered trying to change for her.

"Let's go inside," he said abruptly, cutting off that thought before he could make a fool of himself. "It's getting late."

"All right." Tess slid out of her door and walked toward the lobby. He pulled her suitcase out from the backseat and then caught up with her at the door. He held it open with one hand and quickly followed her inside.

"May I help you?" the desk clerk asked.

"Yes, I need a room," Tess said.

"Actually we'd like two connecting rooms," he spoke up, cutting off Tess's request.

"What are you doing?" she whispered under her breath. "There's no reason for you to stay."

"I'm not leaving, Tess." This was why he'd waited to even bring up the subject. "Don't worry, you'll have your privacy."

"We have two connecting rooms on the first floor, but you'll be facing the parking lot. Is that acceptable?" the clerk asked pleasantly.

"Yes, that would be fine." Declan handed over his credit card and ignored the scowl Tess sent his way. "Thanks."

"You'll be in room 110 and 112. Your rooms will be all the way down at the end of the hall."

"Great, thanks." Declan took one key and handed Tess the other one. He grabbed her suitcase and wheeled it down the hallway toward their rooms.

Tess waited to get away from the lobby before she spoke her mind. "This is ridiculous. There's no reason for you to stay here when you have a perfectly good house to go home to."

"Would you consider going home with me? I have a spare bedroom."

"No, I wouldn't." She crossed her arms over her chest, obviously disgruntled. "I like this location. It's close to church."

Sunday was three days away, but he wasn't going to point that out now. "You may as well save your breath, because if you're not leaving, then neither am I."

She sighed, but he was thankful when she gave up her argument. The clerk had indeed allocated them rooms that were way at the end of the building, overlooking the parking lot which was probably a good thing in case they needed to leave in a hurry.

He set the suitcase down and then used his key to open his door. "Unlock your side of the connecting door when you get in, okay?"

"Hrumph." Tess didn't look pleased as she lugged her suitcase inside, letting the door close loudly behind her.

He went inside his room and then unlocked and opened his side of the connecting door.

Since he didn't have any luggage with him, he decided he'd have to go back to the lobby to get a few bare essentials from the front desk.

By the time he returned with a comb, tooth-brush, toothpaste and razor, he noticed that Tess had her connecting door open about an inch. He set his things inside the bathroom and then hesitantly knocked on her door.

"Come in."

He pushed the door open a bit farther and saw that Tess was sitting in a desk chair reading a Bible. It didn't look like the ones that were normally left in hotel rooms, so he assumed it was hers. "Everything okay?"

"Of course, why wouldn't it be?"

Good point. Why the sudden need to check on her? It wasn't as if there was any hint of danger. "Call me if you need anything."

"I will."

"Good night, Tess."

"Good night, Declan."

He closed her door just enough so that it didn't latch, and then did the same on his side. As he stretched out on the bed, he stared up at the ceiling. Was it possible that Tess was right about faith and church? Did believing in God really bring peace?

For the first time, he wondered if maybe he

would have coped differently after Tony's death if he'd had faith and God to lean on.

But almost as quickly as the thought entered his mind, he pushed it away. After all the trouble he'd caused as a teenager, he was certain he'd sinned too much for God to forgive him. Even his own mother hadn't loved him enough to take him with her when she left his father. Instead, she'd taken Karen, leaving him behind.

Furthermore, he didn't have any business thinking of ways to get on Tess's good side. Granted the more time he spent with her, the more he admired her strength and endurance, but he already sensed she didn't feel the same way about him. And while he knew deep down that it was better that way, he couldn't help wishing that things could be different.

That he was the type of man who really could have a home and a family.

# EIGHT

Tess tried to concentrate on the book of Psalms, which were her favorite, but she was acutely aware of Declan's presence in the room next door. She was oddly touched by the fact that he'd chosen to stay with her, so that he could offer his protection.

She couldn't remember the last time any man had cared about her safety and well-being. Of course, she hadn't been in danger like this before, either, at least not since that disastrous prom date ten years ago.

Declan had stepped up to protect her back then, too. She'd tried to repress her memory of that night, but now the images came rushing back. The way Steve's personality seemed to have changed over the course of the evening from being the nice guy she knew in her physics class to the nasty creep who'd demanded sex from her. He'd been drinking all night from a water bottle that really contained vodka, a fact that she realized far too late.

Steve had gripped her wrist so hard that he'd left bruises that had lasted for a full week. She knew Steve would have forced himself on her, but Declan had shown up and demanded that Steve let her go. When Steve was distracted by Declan's arrival, she'd kicked him and had taken off running. She'd heard someone jogging behind her and had tried to go faster. Soon she realized Declan was the one following her, making sure that Steve didn't try to follow.

Declan had offered to drive her home, and during that time, she'd shared her dream of being a doctor while Declan had informed her he was going into the marines. He'd given her a light, gentle kiss, a moment she still savored. Even though Declan had been the town troublemaker, she'd never felt as safe as she had that night.

Until now.

She gave up trying to read and crawled into bed. But she couldn't sleep. Memories of her eventful day kept crowding her mind. The bomb under her desk, the explosion outside, the crash in Declan's old neighborhood.

Searching for Bobby.

Her phone rang and she bolted upright in bed, her heart hammering wildly. She reached for the device and wanted to weep with relief when she saw Bobby's number. "Bobby? Where are you?"

"Tess, I need help." Her brother's voice was barely a whisper, so soft she had to strain to hear. "I need money. Can you meet me at Greenland Park?"

She swallowed hard, trying to ignore the stab of disappointment. "Where have you been? I've been searching all over for you. Do you have any idea how worried I've been about you?"

There was a slight pause before her brother responded, "I'm sorry…I can explain everything when you get here. Please, Tess, it's important. I need your help."

She closed her eyes, fighting a wave of nausea and a nagging headache. Bobby knew that she didn't like going to Greenland Park, the site of her near rape, but obviously he was in trouble. She was afraid to hear the details, yet she knew she'd have to help him. No matter what. "Okay, where do you want me to meet you?"

"I'll be waiting in picnic area number three. Thanks, Tess."

She barely had a chance to say goodbye before Bobby hung up. Her brother sounded as if he was under a lot of pressure for some reason. She didn't mind giving him money, but she needed to understand what he was involved in and how she could help him get back on track.

He'd skipped school, for heaven's sake. What happened to the earnest young man who'd promised her he'd graduate?

Tess took a deep breath and let it out slowly. She didn't have a car, which left two choices. Call for a cab or wake Declan.

Her first instinct was to go with the cab option, but there was a good chance Declan would hear her. It made her a little nervous to tell him about Bobby's request, because who knew what legal trouble her brother had gotten into? But at the same time, she didn't really want to go to Greenland Park alone at eleven-thirty at night.

Before she could move toward the connecting door, Declan rapped on the frame to get her attention then poked his head inside. "Tess? I heard your phone. Was that Bobby?"

"Yes, he wants me to meet him at Greenland Park. Will you drive me?"

Declan frowned. "Of course, but why does he need us to go to him? Why can't he come here? What exactly is going on?"

"Bobby said he'd explain everything when we get there. I need you to trust me on this." She was afraid to mention the fact that Bobby wanted money. Deep down, she suspected that Declan might share Jeff's philosophy of how to manage a teenager. Her ex had made it clear she was too lenient when it came to her brother, yet she knew that being strict wasn't the answer, either. Of course a happy medium would be nice, but at times like this, she knew that was nothing more than wishful thinking.

"I don't like it," Declan muttered.

She didn't have an answer for that, so she grabbed her purse before following Declan out of the room. He headed outside to where he'd left the car.

Her stomach twisted painfully the closer they came to Greenland Park. Being there at night brought back memories she'd rather forget. She was relieved to be reuniting with her brother, yet at the same time, she'd rather be anywhere else than Greenland Park.

"Where are we meeting him?" Declan asked as he drove into the park's north entrance.

She forced the words through her dry throat. "Picnic area three."

The darkness enveloped them as the towering trees lining the park road blocked out the light from the moon and the stars. From what she could tell, the area was deserted and there weren't any other cars or people that she could see. Soon their headlights flashed on the sign labeled Picnic Three. "Pull over," she urged.

Declan stopped his car and hesitated before he turned off the engine, including the headlights, plunging them in complete darkness. "Maybe we should leave the lights on, so Bobby can see us?" she whispered.

"Not right now. First I need to be sure you're safe. Since we haven't seen Bobby yet, he's either hiding or hasn't arrived. There's no sign of his truck, but for all we know he could have parked elsewhere and is heading over on foot."

She didn't argue, because something about all of this didn't seem quite right. Granted she already knew Bobby was probably in trouble, but still, using the park as a meeting place felt—off.

"We're going to walk across to where those three picnic tables are clustered beneath the oak tree," Declan said. He reached up and fiddled with the dome light, and she was surprised when he removed the tiny bulb. "I want you to stay right next to me, okay?"

She nodded and looped her purse over her shoulder as she opened her door. Her foot hit the curb and she slipped, falling against the side of the SUV with a soft thud. Declan was there in a heartbeat, to steady her.

"Are you okay?" he whispered.

"Yes, I'm fine."

Declan held on to her hand as they gingerly made their way across the grassy embankment toward the three picnic tables. The dewy grass made her running shoes damp as they walked, making sure not to trip over branches or rocks.

She peered through the darkness, trying to catch a glimpse of her brother. Was Bobby hiding somewhere nearby? Was he watching them right now? Was he disappointed that she hadn't come alone?

She shivered and hoped Bobby wouldn't try to do anything foolish, especially since she knew Declan was armed and a highly trained member of the SWAT team. When they reached the middle picnic table, they stood for a while, anxiously waiting for her brother to show.

But he didn't. Where was he? Had he expected her to take more time to arrive? Was he on his way here right now? Or had something prevented him from coming at all?

The latter thought was far too depressing. She sat down on the bench seat of the picnic table, but Declan stopped her.

"Wait," he said in a hushed tone.

She froze while Declan pulled out a small flashlight. He swept the tiny yet powerful beam over the area. There was no sign of anyone hiding nearby, although there were certainly enough trees and brush to hide behind.

She had no idea what he was looking for, but then she heard him suck in a harsh breath.

"What's wrong?" she whispered.

"Look," Declan said in a husky tone. Beneath the picnic table to their left was a small cardboard box. For a moment she didn't understand the significance, thinking that some previous picnicker had left it behind.

"I have to call this in," Declan said in a grim tone. "I think this could be another bomb."

Declan knew that the small cardboard box could be nothing, but ever since they'd arrived in the park his nerves had been on edge. No way was he taking a chance on the fact that this could be yet another explosive.

Using his radio, he called his boss and reported the potential threat. Griff agreed to send his SWAT team and the robot, as this was an isolated device, and the rest of his gear. Feeling better that he had backup on the way, Declan fished out his keys and glanced at Tess.

"Here, I need you to go back to the car and lock yourself in," he said, dropping the keys into the palm of her hand.

"I'd rather stay here with you," she protested.

No way, he didn't want her anywhere near the bomb. He was already worried that it could be ready to blow. "I'll walk you back," he said. "I want you to shut off your cell phone, because we have no way of knowing if this device is on a timer or if it could be detonated remotely. For all we know, someone is out there right now ready to set it off."

"Stay with me," she begged. "At least until your team arrives."

Her concern warmed his heart, even though he knew Tess would be worried about anyone who was in harm's way. "I'll stay clear, but I need to make sure no one else gets too close, either."

"There isn't anyone else here," she protested.

"Tess, you know as well as I do that there are likely a few homeless people roaming around this park. This is my job," he reminded her gently. "You can help me out by locking yourself inside the vehicle. In fact, I'd like you to drive back to the hotel, just in case."

He didn't want to scare her, but for all he knew there was either C-4 or dynamite in that box.

Or nothing at all.

"How will you get back?" she asked.

"Caleb or Isaac will drop me off. Please go. I need to know you're safe."

"All right," she reluctantly agreed. "But promise me you'll be careful."

"Always," he assured her. As she climbed behind the wheel, he realized how hard it must be for the guys' families, sitting at home, waiting for news. He wasn't sure how Noelle, Caleb's wife, managed the stress.

Would Tess be able to do the same?

He shook his head at his foolishness as members of his team arrived. Isaac pulled up first and Declan headed over to grab the bomb gear.

"If this is another explosive, this would be a new record," Isaac muttered. "Three in one day? What in the world is going on? Why is this perp escalating?"

"Good question," Declan said as he donned the heavy protective gear. "I can only hope this is a false alarm."

"No such luck," Isaac mumbled. "The feds will go crazy over this."

Declan silently agreed. They sent the robot in first, but it soon became clear that it couldn't navigate beneath the picnic table. Resigned to doing the task himself, he put on a headlamp and led the way back to where the cardboard box was sitting beneath the picnic table.

Declan knelt a few feet away and used a long device to gingerly lift the cardboard flaps one at a time. When the box was open, he glanced at Isaac. "I'm going to look inside," he said in a muffled tone.

"Roger, Deck," Isaac responded.

Declan slowly eased forward, hoping that there wasn't some perp hiding out, waiting for him to get close enough before he triggered the device. He found himself repeating the prayer Tess had said when he'd worked on the mechanism under her desk.

*Dear Lord, if it be Your will, give me the wisdom and strength to disarm this bomb. I ask for Your mercy and grace. Amen.*

Declan craned his neck forward to see inside the box. His headlamp confirmed his suspicions. There were three sticks of dynamite wrapped together with electrical tape, along with an old-fashioned egg timer wired to the front.

There was only about fifteen minutes left on the timer before it was designated to blow.

He glanced over at Isaac. "Fourteen minutes and counting. I'll take the lead."

Isaac looked as if he might protest, but Declan didn't give him the opportunity. Feeling more confident now that he could see that the device didn't have a remote detonator, he crouched beside it and pulled out his wire cutters.

But as he examined the wires, his usual coolness deserted him. And for the first time in a long while, he realized just how much he wanted to live. Not that he ever had a death wish or anything, but still, he had more to live for now. Not just to bring this guy to justice for the lives that had been lost.

But because of Tess. Because as crazy as it sounded, he wanted a chance to get to know her better. To relate to her on a personal level once all this absurdity had been settled.

"Deck?" Isaac asked through the radio. "Something wrong?"

Declan shook his head, realizing he'd been standing there staring at the bomb for at least two minutes. "No, I'm fine. Twelve minutes and counting."

He cleared his mind and focused on the task at hand. The bomb was rigged in a standard, straightforward format, but he couldn't help thinking that the guy who'd made the previous bombs wouldn't have done something so simple. He gently tugged on the wire that logically would lead to the timer, and then moved on to the next one.

There were slight gaps between the sticks of dynamite, and he caught the barest glimpse of a black wire tucked into the back of the timer. He clipped that wire first and was relieved when the timer stopped.

"Bring me the steel box," Declan said to Isaac. "The timer has been shut down, but I'm not sure which wire leads to the trigger."

"Roger, Deck."

Within minutes Declan had lifted the explosive device and placed it gingerly inside the steel box. Then he and Isaac jointly carried it over to the armored truck. Declan didn't relax until they'd closed the explosive device inside.

"Good job, Deck," Isaac said, slapping him

on the shoulder. "For a minute there, I thought you lost your nerve."

"Never that," Declan assured him. "Just needed to think it through, that's all."

He was embarrassed to admit that he'd taken the time to pray and to contemplate just how much he had to live for. Which reminded him he needed to call Tess. He took out his phone, turned it on, but was stopped by his boss.

"We need to talk," Griff said curtly. "Now."

Declan grimaced. Now that the threat had been neutralized, he knew his boss had several questions: first and foremost, how Declan had come to the park to find the device in the first place. As much as he wanted to talk to Tess, she'd have to wait.

Thankfully, she was likely safe inside the hotel right now. A few more minutes wouldn't matter much.

He followed his boss over to where the rest of the team waited and drew a deep breath as he prepared to give them the rundown on the latest turn of events.

Events that now put Tess's brother smack-dab center in the pool of possible suspects.

After leaving picnic area three, Tess drove slowly through Greenland Park looking for the exit. She caught sight of a blue GMC truck with the letters UTS on the license plate and slammed on the brakes in surprise.

Bobby's truck! He had come after all!

She pulled up behind the GMC but couldn't see anyone inside. Where was her brother? She slid out from behind the wheel and quietly closed the car door behind her.

"Bobby?" she called softly. "It's me, Tess."

She strained to listen but couldn't hear anything other than the rustling leaves and the occasional chirping of a cricket.

"Bobby?" She walked up to the truck, pressing her face against the window to peer inside. Had he fallen asleep?

The interior of the truck was a mess, littered with fast food wrappers and empty soda cans. No beer cans, as far as she could tell, which was reassuring.

But there was no sign of her brother.

She walked around to the front of the truck, looking to see if he was nearby, when she heard something rustle behind her.

"Bobby?" she said once again as she turned around.

She caught a glimpse of a dark figure looming over her seconds before something hard hit her on the head, sending pain reverberating through her skull. Before she could gather her thoughts, darkness claimed her.

# NINE

Tess opened her eyes and blinked, trying to see through the darkness. What happened? Where was she?

Her head throbbed and she quickly found the source of her pain in a sizable lump along her temple. There were twinkling stars overhead and it took a minute for her to figure out that the damp feeling was because she was lying flat on her back on the grass alongside the park road.

She pushed herself upright, swaying a bit as the world tilted chaotically on its side. Bracing her hands on the ground, she looked around, sensing something was missing.

For a moment she couldn't think rationally but then realized Bobby's truck was gone. She frowned and stared through the darkness. The truck had been there, right? She hadn't imagined it, had she? Declan's SUV was parked alongside the road and she remembered parking behind Bobby's truck.

She didn't want to believe that her brother had assaulted her and then had taken off. Despite the tension between them, he'd never hurt her physically. It didn't make sense that he would start now. Staggering to her feet, she belatedly noticed her purse was on the ground a few feet away, lying open. When she crossed over to pick it up, her heart sank as she realized her wallet was gone, along with all the cash she possessed.

Tears burned her eyes as a wave of hopelessness washed over her. Why would Bobby do this? She'd brought the money he'd requested and would have given him what he needed. Why would he have hit her on the head and robbed her?

She fished around in her purse for the car keys, but couldn't find them. Had Bobby taken those, too? She tried to think back to her actions and remembered that she'd held the keys in her hand as she searched for her brother.

Crawling on her hands and knees, she brushed her hands over the damp grass, trying to feel for the keys, which had to be somewhere nearby. But after a few minutes of searching fruitlessly in the dark, she gave up. She struggled back up to her feet and went over to the police vehicle. Thankfully she hadn't locked the doors, so she slid inside and switched on the headlights. But even after she turned on the lights, she couldn't see much in the grass.

Discouraged, she shut the headlights off and climbed back out of the car to walk back the direction she'd come. Her head throbbed more with every step until she felt so sick to her stomach she stopped and sank down onto the grass, curling up in a ball and breathing deeply to fight back the urge to throw up.

She had no idea how long she sat there. It could have been a few minutes or close to an hour, but soon a car approached, the bright headlights cutting through the darkness.

The light made her blinding pain worse, so she ducked her head, shielding her eyes from the glare. It occurred to her that she should run away and hide, but she couldn't find the will to move.

"Tess? What happened?"

Declan's reassuring voice broke through the fog in her head. She glanced up at him as he hovered over her. "I'm…sorry. Lost…the…keys—"

She couldn't finish her thought, but it didn't matter because Declan lifted her in his arms and carried her. She put her head on his shoulder and closed her eyes, giving in to the overwhelming fatigue now that she knew she was safe.

Declan held Tess close, his heart pounding with fear and worry as he headed over to the car.

He didn't understand why she hadn't gone back to the hotel, or why she'd been lying along the side of the road, yards away from the sheriff's deputy vehicle he'd loaned her.

"What happened?" Isaac asked.

"Not sure but I need you to call 911." Declan gently set Tess on the passenger seat, but she slumped forward as if unconscious. "Hurry," he urged Isaac.

He held Tess upright listening as Isaac requested an ambulance for a suspected assault. Declan performed a cursory exam and found a lump along the side of her head.

Two head injuries in less than twenty-four hours couldn't be good.

"Is she okay?" Isaac asked, coming over to where Declan was kneeling beside the car. "Is there something I can do?"

Declan tore his gaze from Tess's pale face. "She mentioned something about lost keys," he said. "She must have misplaced the keys to my vehicle."

"I'll take a look around," Isaac said, pulling out his mega flashlight.

Declan nodded, his attention focused back on Tess. She was breathing okay and he could feel the rapid beat of her pulse, yet she didn't respond when he called her name.

He hated feeling helpless, unable to do anything for Tess other than to wait for the ambulance to arrive.

But then he remembered how he'd prayed when defusing the bomb, secretly amazed at the sense of peace. Why not try that again?

*Dear Lord, thank You for watching over Tess and please heal her wounds. Amen.*

Again he experienced a sense of peace, of rightness that he never felt before. And even though Tess wasn't responding to him, he spoke to her anyway.

"Hang in there, Tess. Help is on the way. I'm right here and I won't leave you. But this time you are for sure going to the hospital to be checked out, so don't even try to argue."

He continued his one-sided conversation until the wail of sirens reached his ears. Within a few minutes the ambulance pulled up just as Isaac jogged back over.

"I found your keys," he announced, holding them up triumphantly.

"Thanks," Declan murmured. He stayed right where he was until the two EMTs pulled their equipment from the back of the ambulance and crossed over to him. "What happened?"

"I'm not sure, but she had a lump along the side of her head," Declan explained.

"We'll take a look. If you don't mind, we'll

need some room to maneuver in order to get her on the gurney."

"Sure." Declan stepped back, watching closely as the two men worked together to examine Tess once they had her safely strapped onto their gurney.

"Declan?"

He jumped forward when he heard Tess's voice. "I'm here, Tess."

Her hand grasped his tightly. "Bobby's truck… was here. All my money's gone."

The implication of what she was telling him sank into his brain. "He attacked you in order to steal the money?"

Her eyes glittered with tears. "I don't know for sure…that it was Bobby," she whispered. "Could have been…someone else."

He ground his teeth, willing himself not to lose his temper. "Try not to worry about it now, Tess," he said in an attempt to reassure her. "We'll keep searching for your brother. Right now I want you to concentrate on taking care of yourself, okay?"

"Okay," she agreed, although he could still see the worry in her pretty brown gaze.

"We're taking her to Trinity Medical Center," the EMT informed him.

"I'll meet you there." As much as he wanted to ride in the ambulance with Tess, he needed to drive so that he would have his car on the off chance they ended up discharging her.

He stood beside Isaac, watching as they loaded Tess into the back of the ambulance.

"Do you want me to come to the hospital?" Isaac offered.

He was touched by the offer but shook his head. "No, but thanks."

Isaac clapped him on the back. "I'll put out an APB for that GMC truck," he offered. "And don't forget Griff wants your report ASAP."

He grimaced. "Yeah, I know."

"Let me know if you need anything else," Isaac said before he headed over to his car. Declan nodded and then jogged the few yards back to where his vehicle was parked. He slid behind the wheel and made a U-turn in the road so he could follow the ambulance.

Griff's report could wait until he'd made sure that Tess was really okay. At least physically. Mentally, emotionally, he knew she'd suffer.

Because her brother was clearly involved in this mess, too. Declan figured Tess was holding on to false hope, that Bobby was really innocent despite all the evidence that was now stacked against the kid. But Declan didn't believe in coincidences. The fact that Bobby called her and asked her to meet him at the same place where a bomb was planted was too much to ignore.

Not to mention the way she was subsequently attacked and robbed.

Declan could only hope that one of his colleagues found Bobby soon, before they stumbled across another bomb.

Because Tess's brother was already facing significant jail time.

He drove to the hospital parking lot and climbed out from behind the wheel. The antiseptic smell of the hospital assaulted him when Declan walked into the emergency department. His uniform was badly wrinkled, but his badge should still be enough to cut through the red tape.

"I need to see Tess Collins," he said to the woman behind the front desk.

"Ah, sure, let me see." She tapped on the computer keys and then nodded. "Oh, yes, Ms. Collins is in room twelve. Go through the doors and it's the last room on the right."

"Thanks." He strode through the double doors and found Tess's room without difficulty, although there was a doctor and a nurse in there, so he waited outside the door while they tended to her.

Tess looked pale and fragile dressed in a hospital gown. Her blond hair was tangled and her amber eyes were closed, her pinched expression betraying her pain.

He was relieved when he overheard the doctor order a CT scan of her head to assess for a brain injury. And he wasn't surprised to hear that they also discussed whether or not she would need to stay in the hospital for twenty-four hours of observation.

Tess would hate staying, but he didn't care. He needed to know she was medically stable, and Tess would likely be safer in the hospital than anywhere else right now.

Once the doctor and nurse left, he went inside and took her hand in his. "How are you feeling?"

"Declan?" She opened her eyes and turned to face him. "Have you found my brother?"

"Not yet, but don't worry. We'll find him." He didn't elaborate more, as he didn't want her to be upset about the fact that the entire police force would be out looking to arrest Bobby.

Her eyelids fluttered closed and her fingers relaxed their grip on his, but he didn't let her go until the radiology staff came to take her for her CT scan. Declan sank into an uncomfortable plastic chair, wishing he had a laptop so he could begin working on his report.

He tipped his head back against the wall and closed his eyes, feeling the effects of the adrenaline crash. He was exhausted and knew Tess must be even more so. She'd been through so much, and had never once complained.

His phone rang, jarring him back to reality, and he grimaced when he saw the caller was his boss. No point in ignoring the call, so he pushed the talk button. "Yeah, what's up, Griff?"

"The FBI wants to talk to you again. How quickly can you get here?"

He closed his eyes and sighed. "I'm at the hospital, and it's well past midnight. Can't this wait until morning?"

"You can't say no to the feds," his boss informed him. "And I need to give them a time frame."

Declan didn't want to leave, but Griff was right: the feds never took no for an answer. He glanced at his watch. "I can be there in ten to fifteen."

"Good." Griff abruptly hung up.

He tucked his phone back into his pocket and scrubbed his hands over the stubble on his jaw. He could use a shower, a shave and a change of clothes. Maybe leaving for a while wouldn't be the end of the world. He could let Tess's nurse know so she wouldn't worry. Besides, he didn't think Tess would be discharged anytime soon.

Decision made, he summoned the nurse into the room, filled her in on his plans and asked her to give him a call if Tess's condition changed. After she graciously complied, he flashed a tired smile and then made his way back outside. There was no reason to be nervous…Tess was in good hands. She probably needed rest and relaxation anyway.

Declan drove back to headquarters, mentally preparing himself for the interrogation to come. He could only imagine what Agents Walker and Piermont would think about this latest turn of events. Was it possible they still believed he was personally involved in setting these bombs? Last time Griff had supported him, but Declan sensed his boss was quickly losing his patience with the lack of viable leads.

Despite the lateness of the hour, the building was brightly lit up, indicating an unusual amount of activity. He parked and headed inside, finding Griff and the two FBI agents waiting for him.

"About time you showed up," Agent Walker groused.

Declan held on to his temper with an effort. "I was at the hospital with a key witness," he said without apology.

Agent Walker scowled, but Agent Piermont offered a smile. "How about we go someplace private to talk?" she suggested.

Griff grunted and headed over to the same interrogation room they'd used earlier that day. Hard to believe that only sixteen hours had passed since Tess had discovered the bomb beneath her desk.

"I could use a cup of coffee," Declan announced. "Anyone else interested?"

"Sure, I'll come with you," Agent Lynette Piermont said, jumping to her feet.

As he poured two cups of coffee, Declan wondered if she always played the role of good cop. Agent Piermont added a good dose of cream and sugar while he sipped his black.

"Long day, huh?" she asked with obvious sympathy.

He shrugged, unwilling to be drawn into whatever game they were playing. "For you, too, I'm sure."

"Tough case," she agreed.

He turned and headed back to the interrogation room, suddenly annoyed with the small talk. He wanted to get this over and done with so he could head back to Tess.

"So you found another bomb, the third in one day," Agent Walker said without preamble.

Declan folded his arms across his chest and nodded.

Agent Walker stared at him, letting the silence drag out for several interminable seconds. Declan held his ground; he knew how to use these same interview techniques, too.

"How was it that you went to Greenland Park in the first place?" Agent Walker finally asked.

Declan took another bracing sip of his coffee before trodding through the same story he'd given Griff earlier. His boss remained silent as he explained how Tess had heard from her brother and gone out to meet him.

"We've run a check on Bobby Collins," Agent Piermont interjected. "Seems he has a couple of disorderly conduct tickets on file."

Declan shrugged, thinking about the disorderly conduct citations he had gotten himself as a teenager. He'd actually done worse things, but was lucky enough not to get caught. Joining the marines would have been impossible if he'd had a significant criminal record. And despite everything, he was glad he'd been given a chance to turn his life around.

"Sounds like this Bobby Collins is now your number-one suspect," Agent Walker said. "You need to bring him in for questioning."

Declan mentally counted to ten before he spoke, keeping his tone even. "And we will, as soon as we find him."

Agent Walker scowled. "If you knew Ms. Collins had a brother, why didn't you put the APB out on him earlier? Maybe we could have avoided this latest bomb if you'd done your job."

Declan glanced at Griff, but his boss's bland expression didn't give anything away. Was Griff siding with the feds? "If you recall from my earlier report, we had a viable suspect, the guy wearing a green baseball cap who was not only seen at the scene of the elementary school, but was literally in the area minutes before the bomb exploded. Are you suggesting that I should have ignored that suspect to follow up on Bobby Collins?"

Spoken out loud, the idea sounded twice as ridiculous. The glimpse of a smile played across Griff's face as the two agents exchanged a frustrated glance.

"So tell me…when did you first decide that Bobby Collins might be a potential suspect?" Agent Walker demanded.

Declan shrugged. "Not until I found the bomb beneath the picnic table at the designated meeting place. There was no reason to suspect him earlier."

"I need to be notified immediately once you have Bobby Collins in custody," Agent Walker declared. "Understand?"

Declan had the ridiculous urge to laugh but managed to keep a straight face. "Of course. Is there anything else? Has your investigation unearthed any leads?"

The agents exchanged another frustrated glance. "We're finished here. Don't forget to turn in your report."

This time it was all Declan could do not to roll his eyes. As if he really needed to be told to do his job? What was wrong with these feds anyway? Surely they had other things to worry about.

He pushed to his feet and turned to his boss. "I'm going to shower and change before heading back to the hospital. Call if you need anything."

Griff gave him a curt nod, and Declan released a breath he hadn't realized he'd been holding as he walked out the door. He went to his locker to get a fresh uniform, and then quickly used the facilities to shower, shave and change.

He felt 100 percent better as he drove back to Trinity Medical Center. The woman behind the desk recognized him from earlier, and waved him through.

As he strode down the hall toward Tess's room, he frowned when he realized there was a man wearing a navy blue jacket and gray dress slacks peering in through the half-closed doorway.

The guy looked familiar and it took a moment to recognize Allan Gray, Tess's geeky neighbor.

"Hey, what are you doing?" Declan called out sharply.

Clearly startled, her neighbor jerked around, gaping at Declan in surprise. Without saying a word, Gray turned and ran off in the opposite direction.

What in the world was Gray doing here?

Spying on Tess? Declan sprinted after him, following as he disappeared through a doorway. Declan covered the distance as quickly as possible, bursting through the same doorway a few minutes later.

But all he saw was a long, empty hallway. There were several doors but he had no idea which one Tess's neighbor might have taken.

Allan Gray had gotten away.

# TEN

Tess faded in and out, unable to keep her eyes open for very long, which made it difficult to keep track of what was happening around her.

But every time she opened her eyes Declan was there, sitting in a chair beside her bed. Reassured by his presence, she let herself drift.

Finally she woke up, feeling as if she could actually stay awake for a while. Bright sunlight was streaming through her window and she stared at the clock on the wall in shock. Two-thirty in the afternoon?

Had she really slept for more than twelve hours?

She struggled upright, wincing a bit as her head protested the sudden movement. Glancing over to where she remembered seeing Declan last, she was disappointed to find the chair was empty.

Of course he'd probably gone to work. After all, twelve hours was a long time to expect him to sit by her bedside. Thankfully, Greenland Elementary was closed so she didn't have to report in. Not that she was in any shape to teach anyway. She lifted her hand to her hair and grimaced at the tangled mess.

A nurse entered her room, looking a bit surprised to find her awake. "Hi, my name is Sally. How are you feeling? I must say, you're looking much better."

"Thanks, I feel better." Tess realized she wasn't in the emergency room any longer but had no memory of being brought to a regular room. "I'd like to get up to use the bathroom."

"Certainly," Sally agreed, coming over to help. "Sit on the side of the bed first, in case you get dizzy."

Tess did as she was told. Sally was right on— the room tilted wildly, but then stopped moving after a few minutes. She braced herself on the bed and remained still, breathing deep and keeping her gaze focused on the bathroom door.

"Are you ready?" Sally asked.

"Yes." Tess hated feeling like an invalid, but she allowed the nurse to assist her into the bathroom. After using the facilities, she insisted on taking a shower and felt much better afterward.

Getting the snarls out of her hair wasn't as easy, and soon she was tired again. She crawled back into bed with a scowl, wondering when the doctor would show up to release her. She was already feeling guilty for being here this long, when all she had really needed was some sleep. And who could blame her after the day she'd had?

"Hey, you're awake," Declan said as he came into the room. He looked amazing with his clean shaven jaw, jeans and button-down denim shirt.

She smiled, unable to hide the fact that she was happy to see him. "Finally, huh? It's good to see you. Any idea when they'll spring me?"

"You're probably going to have to stay one more day," Declan advised. "They were worried about a small head injury they found on your CT scan."

"Really?" She put her hand to her temple, outlining the swollen area gingerly with her fingertips. "It doesn't seem any worse than the lump on the back of my head."

"Two head injuries in one day are serious enough to warrant close observation for a while."

She had no intention of staying here another night, but there was no point in arguing with Declan about that, so she changed the subject. "What did I miss? Have you found Bobby? Has anything else happened?"

Declan shook his head. "No, we haven't found Bobby and the only thing I've done is to write a bunch of reports and be interviewed by the feds."

Her good mood faded at the realization that her brother was still missing. "Did you check to see if Bobby reported to school this morning?"

"Yes, I called first thing. But he didn't show."

Despair nearly overwhelmed her. Where on earth could he be? The only logical explanation was that something bad had happened to him.

"Tess, tell me about your relationship with your neighbor Allan Gray," Declan said, breaking into her troubled thoughts.

She frowned. "What do you mean? We don't have a relationship. He's just my neighbor."

"Has he ever made any romantic overtures toward you?" Declan pressed.

"No, of course not. He offers to help me at times, and we chat if we see each other outside, but that's about it."

"What does he help you with?"

"Neighborly things, you know, like helping me to carry in my groceries or offering to shovel my driveway."

"He's been inside your house?" Declan asked, obviously appalled.

"Only in the kitchen, and it's not a big deal." She shrugged at his stern expression. "Honestly, I rarely take Allan up on his offers because I'm afraid of leading him on, or giving him the impression that we're more than neighbors. I'm nice to him and he's nice to me, that's all."

"So you do sense that he's a little off," Declan mused. "I don't blame you for being wary, since the guy is clearly following you."

Her jaw dropped. "What makes you say that?"

"He was here in the middle of the night, standing outside your room while you were still in the E.R.," Declan explained with a dark frown. "The minute he saw me, he took off. I went after him, but I lost him."

She relaxed and fought a smile. "Allan's not following me. He works as a third-shift security guard here at the hospital. He probably walked by my room and stopped when he recognized me. You're making a big deal out of nothing."

Declan was not amused. "So why did he run off when I asked him what he was doing? Why not come over and talk to me?"

"Maybe because you're scary?"

His scowl deepened. "I'm not scary and I'm telling you, he definitely looked guilty. Don't forget I saw him in my old neighborhood, too, shortly after you crashed. There's something not quite right with that guy and I wouldn't put it past him to plant bombs in the area. For all we know, he's carrying some sort of grudge since high school."

She sobered, thinking about how close she'd come to being seriously hurt when she crashed into the light post after the rock had shattered the windshield. It was strange that Allan would be nearby after that incident, but it had to be a weird coincidence. Because no matter what Declan thought, she couldn't imagine Allan doing something as crazy as setting bombs around the city.

"I'm sure he's not following me," she repeated. "You can't blame the guy for being around while he's working. Do me a favor and find my doctor. I'd really like to get out of here." Seeing Declan's dark scowl, she quickly added, "You know that I need to keep looking for my brother, and I can't do that from a hospital bed."

Flattening his lips, he stared at her for a long moment. "Look, Tess, every cop in the city is looking for Bobby. And they have a much better chance of finding him than you do."

"What?" She did not like the way Declan made it sound, as if her brother was some sort of criminal. "Why? Did you list him as a missing person?"

He winced and averted his gaze. "Not exactly."

A flash of anger burned through her. "You actually think he's guilty of planting that bomb under the picnic table? Come on, Declan, he's seventeen years old! Bobby has no reason to set bombs or try to blow things up. Especially not me!"

"Tess, you have to admit it's possible—"

"No, I don't," she interrupted. "No matter what kind of trouble Bobby is in, he wouldn't hurt me."

"What about the incident last night?" he demanded. "Someone hit you from behind and then robbed you. And you saw Bobby's truck. Why wouldn't he be involved? Clearly he's in way over his head."

"You're way off base. Bobby didn't hit me. It's clear he's in trouble. Maybe his friends turned on him for some reason and took his car and his phone."

"That's ridiculous," Declan scoffed. "You're wearing blinders, Tess. Trust me, I've been Bobby's age. I know what it's like to get mixed up in the wrong crowd. He could very easily have gotten sucked into something illegal."

She bit her lip and tried not to cry, deeply disappointed in Declan's attitude toward her brother. He was just like Jeff, believing the worst. She sniffed back her tears, turned away and pushed the call light, asking for her nurse.

Declan could believe whatever he wanted to, but he'd never even met Bobby. She knew her brother, had raised him for the past six years. Granted Bobby had a couple of run-ins with the law, but deep down, he was a good kid. She believed Bobby loved and cared about her, the same way she loved and cared about him.

Too bad Declan couldn't trust her judgment. And for the first time since yesterday, she felt completely alone.

Declan left Tess's room, battling a wave of frustration. He didn't like having Tess be upset with him, but he didn't understand how she could be so convinced her brother was innocent after all the circumstantial proof that was stacked against him.

He leaned against the wall just outside her room, waiting while the doctor went in to talk to Tess. There was nothing he could do to stop Tess from leaving, and he hated feeling helpless. Why couldn't she do as he'd asked and stay one more night?

Nothing was more important than keeping her safe, other than finding the perp who'd set the bombs. Unfortunately, so far his investigation was nothing more than one big dead end.

Granted, he'd been mostly focused on Bobby and Allan Gray, but maybe it was time to look into that Jeff guy who used to date Tess. He needed to cover his bases, and clearing Jeff Berg would give him more time to focus on the people closer to home.

Declan straightened when the doctor came

back out of the room. "Are you keeping her another night?" he asked.

The doctor shook his head. "No, she's stable and can do the rest of her healing at home. Although she should take it easy for a while."

Declan signed, thinking that task was easier said than done. "Okay, I'll wait until she's ready to leave."

The doctor turned away, presumably to write the necessary discharge orders. Declan entered Tess's room to find her rummaging in the small closet. "Sit down, Tess, I'll get your things for you."

"I'm not an invalid," she said, gathering her clothes to her chest and then turning to face him. "Are you going to drive me back to the hotel? Or do I need to call a cab?"

Okay, she was obviously still upset with him. So why was he still incredibly drawn to her? "Of course I'll drive you back to the hotel. Nothing has changed. I still intend to keep you safe."

She stared at him for a long moment, as if she wanted to say something more, but she simply turned and headed into the bathroom, shutting the door with a loud click.

He lowered himself into an empty chair to wait for her. His phone rang, and he quickly answered it when he saw Isaac's phone number. "Hey, buddy, what's up? Have you found Bobby?"

"Not yet, which is a little odd considering we have everyone on alert. But I wanted you to know that I talked to Allan Gray this morning—he apparently works as a security guard at Trinity."

"Yeah, Tess informed me of that, as well. But did he explain why he took off running when I yelled out at him?"

"Claims he was worried he'd get arrested for some kind of privacy breach."

Declan shook his head, thinking Gray's excuse sounded pretty lame. "Did you ask him where he was yesterday afternoon?"

"Yeah, claims he wasn't anywhere near the corner where Tess hit the light pole, but I did get a good look at his car. He's driving a beige Chevy, so he could have been the guy you saw."

"Yeah, but it doesn't do me any good if I can't prove it." Declan sighed and rubbed the back of his neck. "At this rate, we'll never nail this guy."

"Deck, it's not like you to have a defeatist attitude," Isaac pointed out. "We'll keep poking at the clues and eventually something will turn up."

"I think we need to broaden our search," Declan muttered. "I'm going to look into that Jeff Berg who used to date Tess."

"Isn't he some sort of principal now?" Isaac asked. "Not a likely candidate for a bomber."

"I know, but there was something in Tess's

expression when she mentioned him that sent up a red flag. I get the feeling there's more to that story." The bathroom door opened and Tess appeared, looking pale and drawn. "I have to go, but keep me posted with any updates."

"Will do."

He disconnected from the call and rose to his feet. "Are you ready to go? Do you need to sign paperwork or something?"

"I'll check with the nurse." She pushed her call light and within moments the nurse came in with the discharge papers. After a few minutes Tess was ready to leave, although she flatly refused to use the wheelchair.

Declan walked beside her, ready to catch her if she fell, but it seemed she was truly fine as they made their way down to the lobby. "Wait here," he suggested. "I'll bring the car around."

"All right."

It didn't take long to drive the car up to the entrance where Tess was already walking outside to meet him.

"Are we going back to the same hotel as before?" she asked as they drove away from the hospital.

He nodded. "At this point there's no reason to move locations—the perp likely set up the meeting at the park because he didn't know where you were. I think we'll stay at least one more night, before moving on." He didn't add that the main reason he wanted to stay was so that Tess could get some much-needed rest.

"Good," she murmured. "I'd like to go to church tomorrow morning."

"Tomorrow is Saturday," he said, wondering if the bonk on her head caused her to be confused.

"I know, but there's usually an early morning service every day."

Okay, so she wasn't confused. "That's fine if you want to go, but I'll go with you."

She slanted him a curious glance. "I'm glad. You might find out that you really like it."

He didn't want to burst her bubble. The fact that he'd prayed while he worked on the bomb beneath the picnic table didn't mean that he planned to start attending church every week.

He steered the subject away from faith and church. "I need to know about your relationship with Jeff Berg."

Tess crossed her arms across her chest, immediately going on the defensive. "Why? I told you that he's not involved in this."

"How can you be so sure?"

She turned and stared out her window for several long moments. "We dated, and then he took a new job. That's all there is to it."

He was convinced she was holding back.

"Tess, please. I'm sorry if you think I'm poking my nose in your personal business, but I really need to understand what went wrong between the two of you. If he's innocent, that's fine, because right now I'd like nothing more than to cross at least one suspect off the list."

Tess sighed and shook her head. "There isn't anything to tell."

He'd interviewed enough suspects to know that wasn't true. "If a guy is happy and thinking of spending the rest of his life with a woman, he's not about to look for a new job in another state. Which means that something wasn't right between the two of you."

"We weren't serious," Tess protested. "And Jeff was very ambitious. I knew he wanted a principal position."

She wasn't making this easy. "How was his relationship with Bobby?"

Her flinch was so subtle that he almost missed it. "They didn't get along," she admitted frankly. "But understand that Bobby's attitude didn't help much."

"I'm sure your brother was very protective of you."

She nodded grimly. "Yes, that much is true. But Jeff repeatedly told me that I was too soft on Bobby and that I needed to be stricter with him."

He sensed he was treading on dangerous ground. "Maybe that's just the way he was raised."

"No, that's the way I was raised," she admitted. "My father was strict to the point I used to feel sick to my stomach every time he got angry with me."

He scowled at that. "Did your father abuse you?"

"Not physically, but he was a total control freak. And he didn't hesitate to yell and scream if I stepped out of line. I spent most of my spare time in the library since it was the only safe haven I had to escape the tense atmosphere at home."

Suddenly Tess's reaction to his commands yesterday made sense. "I'm sorry," he murmured. "That must have been rough."

She lifted her shoulder in a careless shrug. "Maybe I was too lenient with Bobby, but I didn't appreciate the way Jeff used to yell at him, either."

Declan tightened his grip on the steering wheel. "Did Jeff do more than yell?" he asked carefully.

Tess pursed her lips together and reluctantly nodded. "I think so," she said in a low voice. "One day I was late coming home and Jeff was already at the house when I arrived. Bobby was sporting a black eye. Jeff denied hitting him but admitted that they'd argued. Bobby wouldn't say anything one way or the other." She released a shuddering breath. "I refused to go out with him that night and Jeff told me that was fine because he'd only come to tell me that he'd accepted a principal position in St. Louis."

Declan found it hard to believe that a man who'd dedicated his life to leading teachers had actually hit a teenager. "Did you report him? Or call the police?"

Tess shook her head. "No, Bobby convinced me not to. He admitted that he'd instigated the argument. I guess I was worried that somehow Jeff's story would change and Bobby would be the one thrown in jail."

Declan nodded, understanding her logic. He remembered several times he'd gotten in trouble just for being in the wrong place at the wrong time. Once the cops tagged you as a trouble-maker, it was difficult to recover.

But this new information swirled around in his head. Was it possible that Jeff was worried Tess had the power to ruin his career? Would he take drastic steps to keep her from talking about what had happened with Bobby? It seemed like a long shot, but he couldn't afford to totally dis-count the possibility.

He pulled into the parking lot of the hotel and

then turned to face her. "Maybe I should pay Berg a visit?"

"I'd rather you didn't," Tess said with a frown. "I don't trust him not to turn everything back to Bobby. Right now it's the word of a principal against that of a troubled teenager. Besides, as much as Jeff turned out to be a jerk, I still can't imagine him running around the city planting bombs as a way to get back at me."

Declan sighed. "You could be right...it does seem to be a bit of a stretch. But someone is trying to hurt you, Tess, and we need to figure out who that could be before he succeeds."

"How do we know that I'm the target?" she asked. "I've been thinking about this a lot, and you're in as much danger as I am. Maybe more, since you're the one who ends up dealing with the actual bombs."

He scoffed at the idea. "I doubt it. The other members of the SWAT team are just as much at risk as I am."

"I heard Caleb and Isaac talking about the fact that you're the main bomb guy. And didn't you work at the minimart when you were in high school?"

He stared at her in surprise. "Yes, but you worked at the custard stand."

"You used to come to the custard stand all the time, even though you didn't buy anything."

Declan swallowed hard. He didn't want to admit that he'd gone there to get a glimpse of Tess.

"Think about it, Declan. What better way to get back at you than to keep planting bombs? And you said yourself, your sister was at the minimart when the bomb went off. Maybe we should be looking at someone who's holding a grudge against you."

Declan didn't know what to say, because he couldn't deny the possibility she was right. All the bomb sites were places where he'd hung out as a teenager.

His gut clenched with dread. What if the only reason Tess was in danger was him?

# ELEVEN

Tess glanced at Declan, who was staring intently through the windshield, clearly deep in thought. She was glad his focus had shifted away from Jeff Berg.

She couldn't believe she'd been stupid enough to go out with Jeff in the first place. Even in the beginning, she hadn't appreciated his stringent attitude toward Bobby. Just thinking of the way Jeff had hit Bobby made her furious all over again. A wave of helpless guilt washed over her. She knew she should have called the police while the bruise darkening her brother's eye was still visible, proof that Jeff had punched him. Even if Bobby had started the fight, she should have defended him.

At the time, she'd been afraid that Jeff would claim Bobby hit him first, somewhere a bruise wouldn't show. And considering the two disorderly conduct citations Bobby had already racked up, she suspected the police would side with Jeff, a respected assistant principal of the local middle school, rather than believe her brother.

Was that the real reason Bobby had skipped school and then disappeared? Because she hadn't done a better job of protecting him last summer? Her cheeks burned with shame at the thought of Bobby blaming her.

It was too late to go back and fix the past; all she could do was to focus on the future. She sent up another silent prayer. *Please, Lord, please keep Bobby safe and show him the way home. Amen.*

"Let's get inside," Declan said, finally breaking the silence.

She nodded and pushed her car door open. She knew she needed to keep looking for her brother, but she was out of ideas as to where to search next.

Had Bobby gone to the church to find her note? She really wanted to go and check, but she worried that going to church tonight as well as going in the morning might cause Declan to be suspicious as to her true motive.

Yet at the same time, she had to know one way or the other. Somehow, she just knew that if Bobby was in trouble, he'd go to the church they'd attended together.

Using her magnetic card key, she opened her

door and went inside. Declan surprised her by following her into the room.

"Are you hungry?" he asked. "We can go out for something to eat."

"Not really, I had a late lunch. But you go ahead… I'm sure you're hungry."

"No, I'm not leaving you here alone," he said stubbornly. "We'll order in when you're ready."

Tess sank down on the edge of her bed, trying to ignore the ache in her head. Sitting here doing nothing didn't suit her.

"I changed my mind," she said abruptly. "I'd like to go back to church tonight, instead of waiting until the morning."

His eyebrows rose. "Okay," he said. "But I'd like to eat something first if that's all right with you. And you should probably take more pain meds, but not on an empty stomach."

She felt bad making him skip a meal, so she gave in. "All right, but all I need is some soup."

He looked as if he wanted to argue, but he shrugged. "Okay, rest for a few minutes while I find somewhere that delivers."

She stretched out on the bed, intending to just close her eyes for a few minutes, but the next thing she knew almost an hour had passed. She had no idea that having a head injury would cause her to feel so exhausted.

"Declan?" she called as she swung upright on

the edge of the bed. The connecting door was open, but she couldn't hear anything.

"I'm here," he said quickly. He strode through the doorway with a tray of food. "I ordered you some chicken noodle soup and scrambled eggs."

"Thanks." She stood and met him over by the small table in the corner of the room. "Did you already eat? Is that pizza I smell?"

"Yeah, I ate already," he said, ducking his head as if embarrassed. "Sorry about the pizza fumes...I hope they don't make you sick."

"I'll be fine," she assured him. She ate the lukewarm soup and eggs while Declan surfed the internet. Her brief nap had restored her appetite.

"Are you sure you're up to a walk to the church?" he asked when she'd finished. "We can wait until tomorrow. I still have some research to do on my laptop and you look as if you could use more sleep."

Tess had to admit it was tempting, but she forced herself to shake her head. "I'd like to go tonight, but you don't have to come along. I'm sure I'll be fine—the church is only a few blocks away."

"I don't want you to go alone, so I'll come with you," Declan said, although she could see the flash of disappointment in his eyes. "Just give me a few minutes to shut down."

"Sure." Tess used the time to freshen up in the bathroom, splashing water on her cheeks in a vain attempt to bring some color to her pale face. Her headache had eased a bit, which she hoped was a good sign.

Declan had carried his computer into his room, returning less than five minutes later. He took her hand as they left the hotel. She told herself that this gesture didn't mean anything other than the fact that he was likely worried that she'd fall flat on her face. But despite her efforts to convince herself otherwise, the warmth of his hand surrounding hers was very distracting as they walked to the church.

"Why is it so dark?" she asked, glancing up at the clouds hovering in the sky.

"Supposed to rain, but not until later."

Tess couldn't help wondering if she was crazy to think Bobby had come to church to find her note. It could be that this was nothing more than a wild-goose chase. Although enjoying the fresh air was nice and refreshing.

If nothing else, sitting in church would help her feel closer to God, at least for a short time.

"Let's try not to stay too long," Declan cautioned as she walked up the stairs to the main doors. "I'd rather not get caught in the rain."

"Are you going to wait in the back?" she asked.

"No, I'm coming up front with you."

To her chagrin, Declan followed her all the way to the front of the church, and she wondered if he would have done this if they had been sitting through a regular service. Somehow she doubted it. As she went into the pew, she brushed her fingers in the corner where she'd left the note, but it wasn't there.

Because the cleaning staff had found it? Or because Bobby had? The possibilities swirled around in her mind and she wanted more than anything to believe the latter.

Declan bowed his head in respect as Tess prayed. He wondered if she was still praying for her brother, and decided that adding something of his own wouldn't hurt.

*Lord, help us find Bobby before it's too late.*

He opened his eyes, feeling a little foolish. What made him think that God would listen to his entreaties? But just like when he'd prayed while defusing the bomb, he felt a sense of peace.

"I'm ready," Tess murmured after what seemed like only a short time had passed.

"Are you sure? There's plenty of time." They'd only been there for about fifteen minutes, and he was worried she'd resent him for making her leave so soon.

"Yes, I'm sure."

He stood and made his way out of the church

pew, waiting for Tess to precede him down the aisle. She stood for a moment at the end of the pew, her head bowed, and he wondered if she was feeling dizzy again.

But before he could ask her, she straightened and stepped away.

Outside, darkness had fallen, mostly because of the dark clouds obliterating the sky. When Tess shivered, he put his arm around her shoulders. To his surprise, she leaned against him as if grateful for the support.

No doubt her headache was back. He wanted to point out that they shouldn't have come, but he stopped himself. The last thing he wanted to do was to act like her father. He understood now that the way she'd rebelled against his edicts before was because of her experiences with her father. Barking orders was a way of life in the marines, but of course he understood that civilians like Tess didn't have to listen.

Somehow he needed to make sure she understood that the only reason he told her what to do was to keep her safe and not that he was a control freak like her father.

Although as soon as the thought formed, he knew that wasn't entirely true. Because he was a man who liked to be in control. He needed to control the things he could because when he went into active crime situations, he was forced to react to whatever was going on.

Tess went tense and he dragged his thoughts back to the present. "Did you hear that?" she asked in a whisper.

He mentally smacked himself in the head for losing his concentration and exposing them to possible danger. He stopped and listened, holding Tess close to his side.

The wind was picking up, whistling through the trees. But he didn't hear anything else. He turned and swept his gaze across the area behind them, but couldn't see much in the darkness.

"I'm sure it was just the wind," he murmured reassuringly. He began walking again, wishing he could pick up the pace. Tess must have shared his sense of urgency because she walked faster than she had on the way over to the church.

A soft thud reached his ears and he reacted without thought, pulling his Glock even as he pushed Tess back into the shadow of the trees. Within seconds he had her crouched behind a tree, while he stood in front of her, wishing he had his night-vision goggles to help penetrate the darkness.

But even though he waited patiently, he didn't see anything move or hear any other sounds. There was absolutely no indication that there was actually someone behind them, tracking their every move. Although he couldn't afford to discount the possibility.

He silently promised himself that if Allan Gray showed up, he'd arrest the guy for stalking. Enough was enough.

But the seconds stretched into a minute, and then two. He hesitated, debating between calling for backup and getting Tess back to the hotel as quickly as possible. They were less than thirty yards away from the bright lights of the hotel.

"Declan, do you see anything?" Tess whispered.

"No." He turned toward her and put a hand under her elbow to help her stand up. "We need to get back to the hotel. Are you able to run?"

"Yes," she answered quickly.

"Stay as close to the trees as you can," he murmured. "And have your key ready."

She gave a jerky nod and he hoped he wasn't making a mistake by running for it. But it went against the grain to call his team when he was armed and they had barely thirty yards to go to reach the safety of the building.

He moved to the right, keeping Tess hidden in the trees. Soon they ran out of tree coverage and without his saying a word, Tess put on a burst of speed, running toward the hotel and jamming her card into the slot in the door.

Keeping right behind her, he mentally braced

for the sound of someone coming after them, but he didn't hear anything and within minutes they were safely inside the hotel. He shut the door behind him, as Tess sank against the wall, breathing heavily.

He reached out for her, intending to offer comfort, but the moment his arms wrapped around her, the embrace went from friendly to intense.

There was no way to know who moved first, but somehow he was kissing her and even more astonishing, she was kissing him back.

Tess clung to Declan's shoulders, losing herself in his kiss. She could have stayed in his arms for hours, but within a few minutes, he gently pulled away and she reluctantly let him go.

She missed his warmth as he stepped back, running a hand through his hair. "I'm sorry, I don't know how that happened."

His apology didn't make her happy. "I'm not sorry, so don't worry about it."

His gaze clashed with hers, and a strained tension rippled between them. This time, she broke the connection by turning away.

"Excuse me," she murmured, escaping into the bathroom. She closed the door and dropped down onto the commode, trying to calm her racing pulse. It bothered her that Declan regretted kissing her, especially since she'd secretly dreamed of being with him again since their first kiss ten years ago.

Even then, Declan had been her knight in shining armor. Saving her from Steve Gains and a potential sexual assault.

Declan had been a year older than her, and of course she remembered seeing him at the minimart and hanging out at the custard stand, his rebellious long hair and black leather jacket screaming defiance. Yet despite his trouble-maker reputation, he'd never been anything but nice and polite to her.

Ironic that all those years ago, she'd been safer with the town rebel than she had been with Steve Gains, the town golden boy. Declan's true person-ality had shown through that night, the way he'd stood up for her and had taken on Steve Gains. She'd realized that much of Declan's tough atti-tude had been a cover for his true nature.

What she didn't know was why.

She gave herself a mental shake. Enough wor-rying about Declan, she told herself firmly. Her brother had to remain her top priority. Her note that she'd tucked into the church pew was gone, but that didn't mean Bobby was the one who'd found it.

She buried her face in her hands, battling a wave of helplessness. What if Declan insisted on switching hotels? Bobby would never find her.

When she'd first heard the noise behind them, she wondered if it could be Bobby, but when the sounds stopped and no one appeared, she figured she was imagining things. But then they'd both heard it again, the barest thud of a footstep. What did it mean? Surely if Bobby had found her, he would have come forward right away?

Unless he was in trouble and was worried about being arrested. She didn't want to think the worst but forced herself to acknowledge that the way Bobby had been missing for the past two days wasn't encouraging.

Maybe it was a good thing that all the police in the area were looking for him. Even if he ended up in jail, at least she'd feel better knowing where he was.

She pulled herself together with an effort, rising to her feet and taking a deep breath before opening the bathroom door. When she stepped into the room, she was surprised to see that Declan wasn't there.

Was he already planning their next move? She racked her brain, trying to think of an excuse that would convince Declan to stay here at least for another night or two.

Long enough for Bobby to find her.

The sound of muted voices wafted through the connecting doorway. Tess rose and walked over, straining to listen.

"I need to know where Allan Gray is," Declan was saying in a low tone. "I think he's following Tess again."

She closed her eyes, despair washing over her. If Declan thought Allan Gray had been stalking them, then for sure he'd make them leave. There was a long pause before Declan spoke again. "So you're saying he's been home this whole time? That it's not possible for him to have waited outside the hospital for us and followed me to the hotel?" His voice rose sharply. "Are you confident enough about this to put Tess's life on the line if you're wrong?"

Several more tense moments of silence passed. Tess clenched her fingers together tightly, waiting for Declan to say something to whomever was on the other end of the line.

"I hope you're right, Isaac," Declan finally said in a weary tone. "And let me know as soon as you hear anything about Bobby."

He disconnected from the call and then lifted his head, catching sight of her hovering in the doorway.

"They still haven't found my brother?" she asked.

Declan grimaced and shook his head. "Not yet."

She nodded, understanding that Declan

wanted to find Bobby just as much as she did. Although for a very different reason.

"Good night," she said, pushing away from the doorway.

"Tess, wait." She paused and turned around to face him. He stared at her for a long moment before he said the words she'd been dreading to hear. "Pack up your things. We need to move to a different hotel."

"Not tonight," she protested.

"We can't ignore the fact that we may have been followed here," Declan pointed out. "What if our perp is out there right now, planting another bomb?"

The stark reality was too much to ignore. She didn't want to leave because of her brother, but was she willing to risk her life?

Or Declan's?

The answer to both of those questions was a resounding no. Tears pricked her eyes and she blinked them away before Declan could see them.

"Give me a few minutes," she murmured. She turned around and went into her own room, closing the connecting door behind her. She needed some time alone.

She sniffed loudly, wiping away the dampness around her eyes. It was so frustrating that she couldn't do more to find her brother.

All she could do was to continue praying for him.

But somehow even praying for Bobby didn't lift the heavy sense of dread that shrouded her. After several long moments, she stood and forced herself to pack her meager belongings together.

There was a faint noise outside, and she frowned and crossed over to the window. There it was again, a slight pinging noise.

She instinctively turned off the lights and waited a few minutes for her eyes to adjust to the darkness. When she heard the third taping sound, she moved the heavy curtain over the window just enough to peer outside.

The window looked over the front parking lot and she scanned the area carefully. But nothing seemed out of place that she could tell. There were several cars parked out front, but none directly in front of her window.

A slight movement caught her eye, and she realized there was a figure crouched near the side of a black truck, mostly hidden in the shadows. She blinked and stared, trying to get a good look at the person's facial features. The way the person was crouched down, she couldn't even tell if it was a male or female.

But then the figure lifted his head and his arm, tossing another pebble at her window.

Relief overwhelmed her, making her knees go weak.

Bobby! Her brother had found her!

# TWELVE

Tess's heart was pounding with anticipation as she opened her hotel room door as quietly as possible and slipped outside. "Bobby?" she called in a whisper. "It's me, Tess. Are you out there?"

"Yes, I'm here." Bobby rose to his feet, and the moment she saw him, she rushed over to throw her arms around him in a huge hug.

"Thank heavens you're safe!" she whispered, clutching him tightly. "You have no idea how happy I am to see you."

"I found your note, Tess," Bobby said.

"I'm glad," Tess murmured. "I've been so worried."

"I'm sorry, sis. I'm so sorry, for everything."

She reluctantly released him and stepped back so she could try to read his eyes. "What happened, Bobby? How much trouble are you in?"

Her brother let out a heavy sigh. "I'm not in as much trouble as Mitch, that's for sure. I thought we were friends, but I guess not." Her brother's tone was bitter.

She couldn't deny feeling glad that Bobby wasn't sticking by his friend Mitch. "Start at the beginning," she suggested. "I went to pick you up from school, but you weren't there..."

"Yeah, we decided to go off campus for lunch and Mitch wanted to skip class the rest of the day. I tried to argue with him, but he wasn't listening."

"What happened next?" she asked.

"He talked me into heading over to the park for a while. Then, out of nowhere, Mitch demanded money to buy drugs. I refused to give him a dime, told him that he needed to go into rehab to get clean. At first, Mitch seemed okay, but as soon as we were about to leave the park, he caught me off guard and slugged me." Bobby raked a hand through his hair, then continued. "Next thing I know, he took off with my phone and my truck. I tried to find him, even went to his house, but he wasn't anywhere...."

"Go on," she prodded gently, trying to keep a tight rein on her emotions. Despite the inner turmoil that she was feeling right now, she needed to remain calm, and composed so he'd tell her the whole story from start to finish.

He cleared his throat. "By this time, it was really too late to go back to class, so I didn't bother. I really thought Mitch would come back and give me the truck keys after he got what he needed, but after an hour or so passed, I knew things were bad. Eventually I walked home, but then I saw your sign on the door, and I've been hiding out ever since."

Tess narrowed her eyes at him. She could see the dark bruises on Bobby's face, but as much as she loved her brother, she couldn't help wondering how much of his account was really true. "Why didn't you call the police?"

Bobby shrugged and stared down at his feet. "At first I didn't want to get Mitch in trouble, and then I was worried that they wouldn't believe me."

Tess tamped down a flash of annoyance. She knew Bobby had a deeply ingrained mistrust of the police ever since his last arrest for disorderly conduct, but he needed to get over it already. Granted the last time he'd been cited he caught a raw deal, as he was truly trying to help a girl who was being threatened by her ex-boyfriend. But of course, the police didn't believe Bobby and ended up giving him a ticket instead of citing the guy who'd started the mess in the first place.

But now the fact that her brother hadn't gone straight to the authorities would make him look bad. And she couldn't deny a tiny sliver of doubt that Bobby had in fact gone along with Mitch, at least in the beginning. "So you weren't the one who knocked me out and stole my money?"

*"What?"* Bobby's shock was too real to be faked. He grasped her arms, staring at her intently. "No! Tell me what happened."

Tess knew her attacker must have been Mitch, hopefully acting alone. "I received a call from your phone and I thought it was you on the other line asking me to meet you at Greenland Park because you needed money. Except when we got there, we found a bomb under the picnic table." Seeing Bobby's eyes widen even farther, she drew a breath and continued. "Declan dealt with the explosive while I went back to his car. I was supposed to return to the hotel, but then I found your truck. When I looked inside, the truck was empty, but someone came up behind me and knocked me out. When I came to, all my cash was gone."

"That jerk," Bobby muttered darkly. "Mitch is going to pay for hurting you. I can't believe he actually mugged you!"

"Don't say things like that," she admonished him. "You're not going to make him pay or do anything else about this. We'll let the police handle it. Which is what you should have done right away. With your statement, I'm sure we can convince the authorities to arrest Mitch."

"I hope so." Bobby shuffled his feet and dragged a hand through his too-long reddish blond hair. "I'm sorry I disappointed you, Tess."

"Oh, Bobby." She sighed and gave him another quick hug. "I know it's been rough the past couple of months, but you have to learn to trust in the system, okay?"

Bobby shrugged, nodded and then changed the subject. "Who's Declan?"

Tess hoped her blush wasn't too noticeable. "He's a friend of mine from high school, who just happens to be part of the Milwaukee County SWAT team. He's been keeping me safe."

"Yeah, I noticed."

"How would you know?" she asked with a frown, trying to understand how her brother had figured that out.

"I saw you two together."

"That was you back there? Following us from church?"

Bobby nodded. "Yeah, but as soon as your bodyguard went into cop mode, I backtracked." Her brother grimaced. "I can't believe you're friends with a cop."

"Trust me, Declan is one of the good guys." She prayed her brother would learn to trust the police. "We'll get through this, Bobby. Always remember that I love you and I believe in you."

Bobby managed a crooked smile. "I love you, too, sis."

She gave her brother another hug, closing her eyes in relief. *Thank You, Lord! Thank You for keeping Bobby safe and showing him the way home.*

Declan glanced at his watch for the fifth time in ten minutes. What in the world was taking Tess so long? He understood she didn't want to leave, but they didn't have a choice.

His goal was to keep her safe. Maybe his imagination had been working overtime on the walk back from the church. It was possible that the only thing he'd heard was the wind whipping through the trees. But he wasn't going to take a chance with her life.

Tess was clearly getting tired of being on the move, and he didn't blame her. He knew that she was still feeling the effects of her concussion. She needed to rest and relax, two things that were difficult to accomplish when you were constantly running from one place to the other.

He straightened, realizing she might have fallen asleep again. Maybe that was why she wasn't ready to go?

He hated the thought of waking her up if she had indeed fallen asleep. Yet she could sleep as long as she needed once they'd gotten settled in a new hotel.

Five minutes, he promised himself. If she hadn't opened the connecting door by that time, he'd have to use his second key to get into her room.

Tess wouldn't be happy to know he actually had a key to her room, especially considering the way he'd kissed her. But since he'd paid for both rooms, the clerk hadn't batted an eye when he asked for one.

He still couldn't believe he'd lost his head like that. The same way he had ten years ago. Granted, their brief kiss the night he'd driven her home after rescuing her from Gains hadn't been nearly enough. He'd thought about kissing her often during those first few weeks after graduation, but then he'd joined the marines and he had bigger things to worry about, like staying alive.

So why had he kissed her again, tonight? He shouldn't have taken advantage of the situation. For one thing, she'd had a concussion. For another, she was his responsibility to keep safe. Getting emotionally involved with Tess was not part of the plan.

Okay, he'd made a mistake by kissing her tonight. But he couldn't allow himself to make another one. Even if Tess had seemed annoyed when he'd apologized for taking advantage of her. Did that mean she'd enjoyed the embrace as much as he had?

*Don't go there,* he reminded himself. *Stay focused.*

He went through his notes one more time, still frustrated by the fact that Isaac had confirmed Gray had actually been at home during the time he and Tess were making their way back from church. But interestingly enough, it appeared that Jeff Berg had taken a short personal leave of absence from his brand-new job.

Had Jeff come back here to exact his revenge on Tess? Declan had instructed Isaac to put out a notice that Jeff Berg was a person of interest in the bombings.

More than five minutes had passed, so Declan took out his spare hotel key and stepped outside. But before he could walk over to Tess's door, he stopped abruptly when he saw she was outside, talking to a young man who towered over her by a good twelve inches.

It took a minute to recognize the young man as her brother Bobby.

"Tess!" His tone was sharper than he intended. "What do you think you're doing?"

She jumped around at the sound of his voice and then stepped protectively in front of her brother, as if Declan were the enemy instead of the guy who'd pledged to watch her back.

His fault, for sounding like a marine drill ser-geant. He mentally kicked himself for reverting to his military mode. But he'd been so surprised to find her outside talking to her brother as if nothing had happened.

"Don't yell at me," Tess said defiantly. "My brother needs help. He's as much a victim of a crime as I am."

*Yeah, right.* Declan reined in his temper. "Let's get inside the hotel, okay? I don't like having you out here unprotected."

"I can protect my sister," Bobby said arro-gantly. "We don't need you."

Declan fought for control, when he really wanted to give the kid a piece of his mind for what he'd put Tess through during his disappear-ing act. He glanced at Tess, hoping she would see reason. "Please, let's go inside and talk, all right?"

"No one followed us here," Tess said wea-rily. "Bobby was the one behind us, so there's no need to worry."

Somehow the knowledge that her brother was the one who'd followed them wasn't exactly reas-suring. "Don't enable him. He needs to be held accountable for his actions," Declan said gruffly. Ignoring her withering glare, he took out his phone, planning to call Isaac. "It's probably bet-ter if we go down to the station to talk."

"What? You can't be serious. Didn't you hear me? Bobby is the victim of a crime!"

"I heard you," he said, striving to remain calm.

"Come on, Tess, let's get out of here," Bobby said, tugging on her arm. "We don't have to stay here with *him*."

"Bobby, wait, just give me a minute, okay?" Tess gazed at Declan as if imploring him to listen. "Don't you remember what it was like to be Bobby's age? To have everyone automatically assume the worst about you? Can't you give him the benefit of the doubt? At least until you've heard his side of the story? Please?"

Declan blew out a sigh, realizing she was right. He did remember what it was like to be Bobby's age, but he'd earned his title of being the town troublemaker and he was pretty sure Bobby had earned his, too. Maybe he could wait a few minutes to hear the kid's side of the story. "All right, fine. But let's talk inside."

"Please, come with me," Tess said to Bobby. "I don't have my car, so it's not as if we can just drive away."

Her brother scowled but gave a tight nod. "Okay, but if he calls to have me arrested, I'm outta here. I'll be fine on my own."

Since that was exactly what Declan had intended to do, he couldn't blame the kid for his response. But he'd made Tess a promise to listen to Bobby's side of the story, so he would. But if the kid tried to lie to them, he wouldn't hesitate to cuff him.

Because whether Tess realized it or not, he was going to do whatever he had to in order to protect her, even from her brother, if necessary.

Tess kept a hold on Bobby's arm, as if he might run off if she let go, while they followed Declan inside the hotel room.

Bobby remained tense and she suppressed a sigh, knowing she would have to be the buffer between the two hardheaded men. Somehow, someway she had to convince Declan to give Bobby the benefit of the doubt.

When the door closed behind her, it seemed the room shrank considerably, uncomfortably crowded with the three of them in there. She gave her brother a nudge toward one of the chairs located near the desk. She sat on the edge of the bed, forcing Declan to take the chair next to Bobby.

"Bobby, explain everything you told me earlier to Declan," Tess said, breaking the silence.

He repeated his earlier story, and to his credit Declan didn't interrupt. When Bobby finished, she wasn't surprised when Declan went back to clarify a few key points.

"So Mitch is the one who assaulted Tess," he surmised.

"I didn't know anything about that," Bobby said with a frown. "He had no right to go after my sister. If I had known his plan, I would have called the police."

"But you didn't," Declan reminded him.

Bobby exhaled sharply. "No. I know I should have, but you don't understand what Mitch has been through. His mom has...issues."

Tess exchanged a glance with Declan, and he nodded, obviously remembering the way Mitch's mother had been drunk when they stopped by. "I know, Bobby," she said softly. "I went over to Mitch's house to try and find you."

Bobby's face flushed with anger. "You shouldn't have done that, Tess. You have to stay away from there. It's a really rough neighborhood."

She silently agreed, remembering the rock that had shattered her windshield. Was Mitch the person responsible? Or someone else?

"Where were you Thursday evening?" Declan interjected. "That's when Tess went to Mitch's house looking for you, but someone threw a rock at her car, causing her to crash into a light pole. She's lucky she wasn't seriously hurt."

Bobby scowled and jumped to his feet. "Are

you accusing me of hurting my sister?" he asked defensively.

Declan raised a hand. "Calm down, Bobby. I'm not accusing you of anything. I was just wondering if you were still with Mitch close to that time, that's all."

The teenager's anger deflated as quickly as it had flared. "The last time I saw Mitch was roughly two-thirty in the afternoon. By Thursday evening, I was back in Greenland Park, hiding out and trying to figure out what to do next."

It broke Tess's heart to think of her brother being all alone without friends or family to help him out. Why, oh, why hadn't her brother contacted the police?

"I believe you," Declan said.

Bobby's head snapped up, his gaze surprised. "You do?"

"Yes, I do. There's no way you'd purposefully harm Tess. The only thing I don't agree with was your decision to avoid going to the police." He pulled his phone out of his pocket. "I'm going to call one of the guys from my SWAT team to put out an arrest warrant for Mitch. Will you provide an official statement about the way he stole your phone and your car?"

"Yeah, I'll give you a statement. But aren't you going to arrest him for assaulting Tess?" Bobby demanded.

"Yes, but we still need more proof to make those charges stick," Declan explained. He started to make the call, but then stopped. "Bobby, did you ever see Mitch building a bomb?"

"What?" His eyes widened in alarm. "No, why? Do you think he's the one setting the bombs?"

Declan shrugged. "Anything is possible. What's the rumor mill at the high school? Is anyone taking responsibility for the bombs? Or maybe bragging about them?"

Bobby slowly shook his head. "No, although a few of the kids made smart-aleck comments about how it would be nice if the bomber would hit the high school so we wouldn't have class."

"What about any kids in the chemistry class?" Declan asked. "Any of them say anything about how easy it would be to make a bomb?"

"Nah, I didn't hear anything like that, but I took chemistry last year, so I wouldn't have been in there to hear anyone bragging or talking about it."

Tess spoke up. "Bobby, if you know anything at all, please tell us." She gave him an imploring look. "Who was the kid who mentioned wishing classes would be canceled?"

"Ricky Jones, but he's not smart enough to plant bombs. He just talks big, that's all."

"We might have a little chat with him anyway, just in case," Declan said as he rose to his feet. Tess noticed a wince flash over Bobby's face and knew her brother wouldn't have given a name if he'd known that Declan was going to interrogate the kid. He called Isaac, but the call must have gone to voice mail since Declan only said, "Call me back," before hanging up.

"This is really serious, Bobby," Tess said in a low voice. "People have died. The police have to investigate every lead."

"I guess," her brother muttered. "You can't blame me for not wanting to be a snitch."

"I can blame you if you don't tell us something that could help arrest this person," Tess countered.

Her brother sighed. "Okay, okay. I hear you."

Declan swung back around to face them. "Tess, are you ready to go?"

"Go where?" she asked. "I thought we could stay since Bobby was the one who'd followed us from the church."

"There's not a lot of room here, and rather than get a third room, I think it might be best if we all go back to my place."

Tess hesitated, instinctively wanting to squash Declan's offer. But she had her brother's safety to consider. Just the thought of Bobby being alone in his own hotel room caused her stomach to clench in fear. She wouldn't put it past Bobby to disappear again if he somehow thought Declan was turning against him.

"If Tess wants to stay here, then that's what we should do," Bobby chimed in, automatically siding with Tess. She was touched by his loyalty.

Declan didn't say anything but kept his gaze centered on her. "Tess? I promise we'll get to the bottom of who's planting these bombs. But I need you to hang in there with me, at least for a little while longer."

She trusted Declan, and maybe Bobby needed to realize just how much the police could help them. "You're right, going back to your place would be easier," she acknowledged. "Thanks for the offer."

"You're welcome."

Bobby looked as if he wanted to argue, but she narrowed her gaze and shook her head. "Don't, Bobby. I've had a long day and I just want to get some rest."

"Does your head hurt?" Declan asked softly.

"Not too bad," she hedged even though the dull pounding was back.

"The doctor told you to take it easy," Declan reminded her. "You should have stayed in the hospital another day."

"Hospital?" Bobby's voice rose in alarm. "You didn't say anything about being in the hospital!"

"I'm fine, it's just a concussion." She glared at Declan, annoyed that he'd worried her brother with that detail. "All I need is to rest."

"Listen, Declan, you have to find a way to make Mitch pay for what he did to Tess," Bobby said harshly. "That's ridiculous that he hurt her bad enough to send her to the hospital. I can tell you what drugs he's been taking and where he gets them. Maybe that can help you track him down."

Declan nodded. "That would help. I'd like nothing better than to find a way to prove Mitch assaulted Tess, and we can talk more about that later. First, I want to get you both someplace safe. Tess is still in danger from someone planting bombs around the city, and until we know for sure that Mitch is or isn't involved, we can't afford to get complacent."

"Crazy. This is just so crazy," Bobby muttered. "I can't believe someone actually has it out for my sister. Tess doesn't have any enemies, well, except for that stupid ex-boyfriend of hers. He was a jerk."

"Jeff Berg, right?" Declan asked. When Bobby nodded, he added, "Yeah, I'm checking him out, among others. We've found three bombs near Tess, and the others had been planted in places she used to work or hang out in." Declan frowned. "Way too much of a coincidence to ignore."

"I appreciate you watching out for my sister when I wasn't able to," Bobby said solemnly. "She deserves the best."

"I agree," Declan replied. "And I promise I'll protect her with my life if necessary."

Tess felt a tiny flutter in the region of her heart as she watched Bobby and Declan talk, pulling together as a united front in order to protect her. She was glad Declan had dropped his overbearing I'm-in-charge cop attitude, and that he was actually treating Bobby like an adult who had something to contribute. Far different from the way Jeff had treated her brother, and she was ashamed to think she'd dated Jeff for three months when he clearly didn't deserve one ounce of her attention.

Now watching Declan converse with Bobby gave her hope, especially since Declan connected with her brother in a way Jeff never had.

And for the first time in a long while, she found herself believing her brother would be okay. At least if they could get through this nightmare. Bobby would graduate from high school and hopefully then go to college or at least a technical school program. She needed to believe he would have a good future ahead of him.

And she knew that with Declan as a role model, anything was possible.

# THIRTEEN

Declan glanced in the rearview mirror at Bobby and Tess in the backseat of his truck as he headed for the highway. She was leaning against her brother, looking relaxed and happy for the first time since he'd been called to disarm the bomb that had been planted beneath her school desk. Despite his earlier annoyance, he was sincerely glad that Bobby had tracked them down at the hotel, although he hadn't been thrilled to hear how Tess had actually left a note in the church stating her exact location. Still, he couldn't deny that her plan had worked. And the kid's concern for his sister rang true, he found himself honestly believing Bobby's story. He planned to call off the arrest warrant on Bobby and put the APB out on Mitch Turner instead. Granted, he'd have to convince the feds, but there would be time to clue them in later.

Maybe now he could focus the investigation

on finding Mitch and the bomber. Not necessarily in that order.

He took a long, winding route to get to his place, making sure no one followed them. The closer he came to his neighborhood, the more vigilant he became. About three blocks from his house, he stopped at a red light near a corner gas station. Glancing over, he noticed a beige sedan, much like the car he'd seen Allan Gray driving, parked in front of a pump. A man was in the process of opening his gas tank and Declan peered through the darkness, trying to get a glimpse of the guy's face. When the man turned and looked up directly at Declan's truck, a chill snaked down his spine.

Allan Gray. The instant their gazes clashed, Allan looked away, hunching his shoulders and keeping his back toward the street as he pumped gas.

The light turned green and Declan pivoted the wheel to the right, going the opposite direction he'd originally intended. He went past the gas station and was tempted to turn around and go back to confront Gray, but held back because he had Tess and Bobby with him.

But what was Gray doing on the opposite side of town from where he lived? Trinity Medical Center was located in the general area between the gas station and Gray's house, and there were service stations every couple of blocks scattered around the city. So there was no need for Gray to drive so far out of his way to fill up his tank.

Unless Gray had somehow managed to figure out where Declan lived and had been watching his house? He clenched his jaw and tightened his grip on the steering wheel to control the flash of anger at the thought.

"Declan? What's wrong?" Tess asked.

He tried to relax his facial expression, secretly amazed at how Tess was so in tune to his feelings. After a moment he admitted, "I saw your neighbor Allan Gray at that gas station."

"Really?" She swiveled in her seat in an attempt to catch a glimpse, but the station was well behind them by now. "Must be a coincidence."

He didn't believe in them but didn't bother pointing that out since there was no reason to scare Tess any more than absolutely necessary. Yet he needed her to be hyperaware of her surroundings just in case Allan Gray was the man guilty of setting bombs around the city.

"Allan?" Bobby echoed in surprise. "You mean our weird neighbor? That Allan?"

Declan met Bobby's gaze through the rearview mirror. "Yeah, why? Do you know something about him?"

Bobby squirmed in his seat. "I know he has a crush on Tess," he finally admitted.

"How do you know that?" she asked incredulously.

"Come on, Tess, he asks about you every single time he sees me. 'Where's Tess? How is she doing? Is she still seeing that Jeff guy?'" Bobby shrugged. "I knew he wanted to ask you out, but I think he was afraid of being rejected. He seemed harmless, so I didn't think too much about it."

Declan knew his initial instincts about Gray were right. "I don't think he's harmless. Is he obsessed enough to follow Tess?"

Bobby slowly nodded. "Yeah, I could see it. I caught him watching her from his window once. I confronted him, but of course he denied it. I let it go, figuring it was good enough that Allan knew I was onto him."

"Why didn't you tell me?" Tess asked in exasperation.

"I didn't want you to be creeped out about it," Bobby said defensively. "I didn't think he was dangerous."

"I'm not so sure," Declan said in a low tone. "I don't like the way he keeps turning up when least expected. I need to get Isaac and Caleb to help me follow him a little more closely. There's something off about that guy and his bizarre fascination with Tess."

"I'll help," Bobby volunteered.

Declan hesitated, not wanting to alienate Tess's brother, yet at the same time, he didn't need a teenage amateur to mess things up. "What I really need from you, Bobby, is to help me protect Tess. I can't be with her 24/7, especially when I'm called away for SWAT team business. I feel much better knowing that you'll be there, watching over her."

Bobby looked a little disappointed, but then he nodded. "You can count on me to help keep my sister safe."

"Good." Declan drove around the block twice before turning into his driveway. "Don't get out until the garage door has closed," he cautioned as he pulled inside.

Bobby and Tess waited until it completely closed behind them before they slid out of the truck. Declan led the way inside, turning on the small kitchen light over the sink and gesturing for them to sit at the table, which was out of sight from the main living area.

"I need for the two of you to stay low, especially at night when it's dark outside. I don't want anyone watching from outside to see you."

Bobby surprised him by nodding in agreement. "It's a good idea. We'll stay well hidden."

Tess looked less than thrilled. "It's going to be hard for us to find our way through a strange house in the dark."

"I'll help you and since it's late anyway, you two should probably get some sleep. We can discuss this more in the morning."

Tess reluctantly agreed. Declan led the way upstairs to the second floor, with Tess and Bobby behind him. He turned on the bathroom light so that they could at least see where the bedroom doors were located.

"My twin nieces usually share this bedroom here," he said, indicating the room off to the left. "There are two beds in there and I think it's best for the two of you to stay together at least for tonight."

"Sounds good," Tess agreed in a weary tone. She looked pale and drawn and he knew her head must be hurting her, even though she never once complained.

He resisted the urge to pull her into his arms for a reassuring hug. The kiss they'd shared just a few hours earlier was way too fresh in his mind.

"Come on, Tess. You can have first dibs on the bathroom," Bobby said, urging his sister forward. "Good night, Declan."

"Good night." Declan headed back downstairs. He waited a few minutes while Tess and

Bobby got settled before grabbing his truck keys and slipping out to the garage.

He intended to find Allan Gray. It was about time he turned the tables on who was following whom.

Tess woke abruptly from a sound sleep, her heart pounding with fear. She couldn't figure out if she'd dreamed the noise or if she'd actually heard someone moving around in Declan's house.

She glanced over to see Bobby was sprawled on the twin bed against the opposite wall of the room. He was sound asleep and snoring softly. She relaxed a bit, glad that the noise, if she'd really heard it, wasn't from Bobby leaving. But what had made that sound?

Tess silently crept out of bed and made her way to the hallway, feeling along the wall as she went. There weren't any lights on downstairs, and she paused at the top of the stairs, straining to listen.

Was someone in the house? If so, she needed to get Declan, but she didn't want to wake him up in the middle of the night if the noise she'd heard was nothing more than her overactive imagination.

She didn't hear anything beyond the beating of her own heart and she slowly relaxed. But now that she was up, she realized she was incredibly thirsty, so she slowly descended the stairs, wincing as one of them creaked loudly beneath her foot.

Just as Tess reached the bottom step, a dark shadow loomed before her and hard hands grabbed her shoulders, causing her to let out a squeak of alarm.

"Tess? What are you doing?"

It took a minute for Declan's familiar voice to register in her mind. "Me?" she asked in a whisper. "You're the one who woke me up by making noise down here!"

"You shouldn't have come down here alone," he muttered. His hands loosened but didn't release her and she enjoyed the warmth of his touch, wishing she could make out the expression in his eyes.

"I wasn't sure if I had imagined it or not," she admitted.

"I'm sorry, I didn't mean to wake you."

She put her hand on his chest, realizing that his clothes were slightly damp. Was it raining outside? Had the noise she'd heard been the garage door closing? "Where did you go?"

There was a long pause before Declan answered, "I went looking for your neighbor."

She was surprised at that. "Did you find him?"

"Not right away. First I went to his house, but

he wasn't there. Then I came back to make sure he wasn't hanging around watching my place. He wasn't in the vicinity, but I eventually found his car in the parking lot of the hospital. I called the hospital—he's working the graveyard shift tonight."

She wished he'd get over Allan Gray already. "I know you suspect Allan, but I really don't think he's the one setting bombs," she said. "He's smart, but not the destructive type."

She heard Declan sigh and when he dropped his hands from her shoulders, she immediately missed his touch. "You could be right," he murmured. "But I still think it's odd that he's always around, even in areas where he shouldn't be."

She rubbed her hands over her bare arms, feeling the chill in the air. "Maybe, but like I said, I can't see Allan as a big threat."

"Don't underestimate him, Tess."

Declan's serious tone made her shiver. "I won't." She moved to step around him, but his hand shot out to clasp her arm, stopping her.

"Where are you going?" he asked.

She rolled her eyes. "To get a drink of water, if that's okay with you."

"Oh, sure. No problem."

Declan followed her into the kitchen and she felt a bit self-conscious as she filled a tall glass of water from the fridge. She downed half the glass and then took it with her to head back upstairs.

Declan hovered nearby as she paused outside the doorway of the spare bedroom. "Good night," she whispered.

"Good night," he echoed.

She put her hand on the doorknob but then turned back toward him. "Declan? Thanks for believing in Bobby and for being so nice to him."

"He's a good kid at heart," he said gruffly. "And I can't deny he reminds me of myself at that age."

She smiled. "You weren't as tough as you wanted everyone to believe."

"I was tough," he protested. "I only showed my softer side with you."

There was a strange intimacy in the air and Tess wanted to reach out to Declan, to tell him how much she was starting to care for him, but he stepped back, abruptly breaking the moment. "See you in the morning," he said, before turning and walking into his room.

She sighed, wondering if the attraction she felt was one-sided. Was he avoiding her on purpose? Maybe, since Declan had been the one to break off their kiss.

She needed to keep her emotions in check. Declan was just being nice to her...nothing more. It would behoove her to remember that, because there was no point in setting herself up for a broken heart.

Sunlight pouring through the window woke Tess the following morning. She blinked, and then sat up when she realized the other bed was empty and she was alone in the room.

For a moment panic seized her by the throat, but then she heard the muted sounds of voices coming from downstairs. Bobby was still here; he hadn't left.

She closed her eyes and sent up a quick prayer of thanks to God for bringing her brother home. She headed into the bathroom, grateful that her headache was almost completely gone. A hot shower and change of clothes made her feel like a new person.

The scent of bacon and eggs made her stomach growl and she went down to the kitchen, pleasantly surprised to find Bobby and Declan huddled around a laptop computer, obviously working, their empty plates evidence of a shared breakfast.

"Hey, sis, how are you feeling?" Bobby asked when he saw her.

"Much better," she admitted.

"Are you hungry?" Declan asked with a smile. "Your brother offered to cook this morning."

"There's plenty of bacon left…how would you

like your eggs?" Bobby asked, jumping to his feet. "Scrambled? Over easy?"

She was taken aback by the offer, since her brother had never bothered to cook when it was just the two of them at home. "Over easy would be awesome."

"Coming right up," Bobby said, heading over to the frying pan sitting on the stove.

Bemused, she sank into a chair next to Declan. "What are you guys working on?" she asked.

"Bobby was giving me information on Mitch Turner," he said, pointing to the computer screen. "Here's his social media page, where he has several photos where he seems to be under the influence."

"Doesn't he understand that anyone can see this stuff?" she asked, frowning at a terrible shot of Mitch looking completely stoned.

"These photos can only be seen by his friends, but yeah, it's crazy that he puts it all out there."

"Tell her about my truck," Bobby said from the stove.

"You found it?" she asked hopefully.

"Yeah, it was left abandoned and out of gas at the end of a dead-end street, not far from Greenland Park," Declan said. "We have the crime scene techs going over it now, looking for hair, fingerprints, et cetera."

"That's wonderful news!" Tess exclaimed. "I'm sure Mitch left something incriminating behind."

"Yes, but that's still a long ways from proving that he's the one who assaulted you," Declan cautioned. "Remember that Bobby and Mitch left the high school together in the truck, so the evidence would have to be something more than just fingerprints or hair. But it's a step in the right direction."

Her brief flare of hope died as she realized Declan was right. They needed something more than just proof that Mitch was in the truck. "What if they found hair and fingerprints on the steering wheel? Wouldn't that indicate that he was driving?"

"Yes, but it's still his word against Bobby's. Don't worry, we'll get him."

"Your eggs are almost finished, Tess," Bobby said. "Do you want toast, too?"

"Sure." She couldn't help thinking that Bobby's new helpful attitude had to be the direct result of being around Declan. She'd done her best in raising Bobby after their parents' deaths, but clearly having a man's influence meant more than she'd realized. Especially a guy like Declan.

Bobby handed her a plateful of eggs, toast and bacon. "This looks delicious, thanks so much."

Bobby's ears turned red and he shrugged off her gratitude. "It's no biggie."

She let it go, sensing he was embarrassed and maybe he hadn't wanted Declan to know that cooking breakfast was not the norm.

"Do you know this guy standing next to Mitch?" Declan asked abruptly.

She leaned forward, trying to get a look at the photo. Bobby sat down on Declan's other side. "Yeah, that's Ken Rogers. He graduated last year," her brother said.

"He's wearing a green baseball hat," Declan said, glancing over at Tess. "Do you think this could be the same guy you saw near the maple tree at the school parking lot?"

The bite of toast lodged in her throat and she swallowed hard before leaning over to look intently at the picture. "I don't know," she admitted. "Ken's hat has a Green Bay Packer emblem on the front, but I think the other guy's hat was plain."

"Here, look at these photos again," Declan suggested. She stood next to him, surprised to see that several of the close-up shots that Nate had taken from the surveillance camera were uploaded on his computer.

It wasn't easy to concentrate on the photos with Declan's musky scent filling her head, but she did her best. "He's not the same guy, I'm almost sure of it," Tess said. "See this picture? There's no emblem on the front of his cap, and you can see that his hair is brown or dark blond, not nearly as dark as the kid standing next to Mitch."

"Okay, you're right," Declan acknowledged. "If only we could get one solid lead on this guy."

Tess reluctantly returned to her seat to continue eating, while Bobby and Declan went through the photos from the crime scene. She was secretly relieved when Bobby didn't recognize the suspect, either.

Declan's phone rang, interrupting them. "Yeah, Isaac, what's up?"

There was a brief pause before Declan shot to his feet so fast he knocked his kitchen chair over. "Really? I'm on my way."

"What's wrong?" Tess asked.

"I have to go. They arrested Mitch Turner," Declan said excitedly. "This could be the break in the case we've been looking for."

"Can I come with you?" Bobby asked.

"I need you to stay here with Tess." Declan picked up the chair he'd knocked over and glanced between the two of them. "I don't like leaving you here alone, but hopefully this won't take long. I'll be back as soon as possible."

"We'll be fine," Tess assured him, standing next to Bobby.

"I hope he confesses to assaulting you," her brother muttered. "He needs to pay for that."

Tess couldn't stop herself from reaching out to gently squeeze Declan's arm in lieu of hugging him. She didn't say anything to stop him from going, but she had a bad feeling that Mitch could easily turn everything around onto Bobby. She could only hope that Declan would find a way to get to the truth.

# FOURTEEN

Declan watched as Isaac questioned Mitch Turner about the events that took place over the past few days. Mitch looked pretty bad—he was pale, sweaty and shaky, and Declan figured the kid was on the verge of going through withdrawal from whatever drugs he'd been taking.

"Tell me again how you ended up with Bobby Collins's phone?" Isaac said patiently.

Mitch shifted in his seat and tapped his fingers on the desktop. "Bobby gave it to me. Just like he loaned me his truck. He's lying if he's telling you something different."

"So where's Bobby now?" Isaac asked. "Why did he leave you with his stuff?"

Mitch looked confused for a moment and it was clear to Declan that the kid's brain wasn't firing on all cylinders. "Uh, he had to go home. His sister told him to come home."

"How did his sister do that?" Isaac asked. "You had his phone, so how did he talk to his sister?"

"I gave him his phone when she called."

"And when was that?" Isaac murmured, leaning back in his chair.

"I don't remember." Mitch glanced around as if looking for a way out.

"And how did Bobby get home?"

"I drove him."

"See, that's where I have trouble with your story," Isaac said with a puzzled frown. "Why would Bobby let you drive him home, leaving him without his truck or his phone? Doesn't he normally drop you off at your place?"

"Yeah, but this was different." Mitch shifted again and his finger tapping became more pronounced. "I needed a favor."

"You needed to buy drugs."

Mitch nodded but then caught himself. "No way, man, that's not true."

"I have to tell you, you don't look so good," Isaac continued. "Are you sure you're feeling all right?"

"Yeah, man. I'm fine." Mitch swiped away a trickle of sweat rolling down the side of his face. "Maybe I am sick. I have the flu. Yeah, that's it. I'm sick with the flu. I need to go home."

Declan blew out a frustrated breath. Even if the kid did confess to assaulting Tess, a decent lawyer would get him off if he was indeed going through withdrawal. They'd be better off getting

Mitch admitted to the hospital and talking to him again when he was sober.

"Pretty sad, huh?" Caleb asked from beside him.

Declan nodded, humbled by the fact that he'd narrowly escaped ending up just like Mitch Turner. Joining the marines had been the best decision he'd made. Without the discipline of being in the service, he didn't think he'd be where he was today. "Yeah, his mother is an alcoholic, too, so the deck was pretty much stacked against him."

Caleb grimaced and shook his head. "Raising kids these days is scary. I'm already worried about Kaitlin's future."

Declan glanced at him in surprise. Caleb's six-year-old daughter was adorable, so why on earth would he be worried? "I'm sure Kaitlin will turn out just fine."

"I hope so," Caleb muttered. "It kills me to see how many kids' lives are destroyed by drugs. And they're getting hooked younger and younger. Noelle insisted on putting Kaitlin in a private school, and I'm glad we did. I'll take all the help I can get."

"I hear you." Declan tried to ignore the tiny flash of envy at Caleb's life with his new wife and daughter. His buddy had narrowly escaped being wrongly imprisoned for murder, so Caleb certainly deserved to be happy.

Declan glanced at his watch, unwilling to leave Tess and Bobby alone for too long. "I need to get back. There isn't much more to do here, since Mitch isn't in any condition to be interviewed. He probably needs to get to the hospital sooner than later."

"I agree. We found drugs in Mitch's pocket, so we can arrest him on possession for now. He also had a good two hundred in cash on him. We should be able to add a charge for intent to sell."

It wasn't as good as getting him for assault, but Declan was willing to take it. For now. "We need to get a warrant to search Mitch's house. There's a chance he might have had something to do with the bomb that was found in Greenland Park."

"Isaac already has a team out there checking it out," Caleb assured him. "Do you have any other leads yet?"

"I still think Allan Gray is involved," Declan admitted. "He's obsessed with Tess, and I think he's been following her. And there's always Jeff Berg, too. I'm still trying to figure out why he took a leave of absence from school."

"I'll work on the Jeff Berg angle," Caleb offered. "I know Isaac was trying to keep an eye on Allan Gray, as well. You're not in this alone,

Deck. Griff told us about the feds, and I just want you to know we're here for you."

"I know and I appreciate the help." Declan knew he was lucky to have friends like Caleb and Isaac. "I don't suppose the feds have come up with anything useful yet, have they?"

Caleb shook his head. "Not that they're willing to share."

That figured. The FBI tended to keep their information to themselves. "All right, call me if anything changes."

"Will do."

Declan headed back outside to his truck, anxious to get back to his house. The thought of Tess and Bobby waiting for him made him think about what it might be like to have a family of his own.

Ridiculous to go there. He'd made a conscious decision not to have a family because he was too much like his father to take the risk. Yet somehow that reason didn't seem good enough anymore. Granted, he'd lost his head when his buddy Tony was shot and killed right next to him, but that was four years ago now, and he hadn't had a drop of alcohol since.

Would that change if he was in a relationship? He didn't want to think so but was afraid to hope.

Why was he even thinking about this? There

was no guarantee that Tess would be interested in him. She deserved someone better, that was for sure. Not Jeff Berg or Allan Gray, but there had to be plenty of single men who'd be interested in her.

Still, the very thought of Tess being with Isaac or Griff or any of the other single guys from the SWAT team didn't sit well with him, so he forced himself to stop thinking about Tess as a woman he was interested in.

Tess was in grave danger. He needed to stay focused on that fact. But right now he was fresh out of new leads. He'd really hoped that Bobby might recognize the guy with the green ball cap, but so far the guy was still a mystery man.

He drove home, intending to do more research. They needed a break in this case soon, before another bomb was set and more innocent lives were put at risk.

Tess finished cleaning up the breakfast dishes and then went back to the kitchen table, to review the photos on Declan's computer again. She went through each of the images, slowly and deliberately. The guy in the green ball cap still seemed familiar. Why couldn't she place him?

She rubbed her hand over her eyes and pushed the laptop away. Maybe she needed to stop trying so hard to remember. Since they hadn't gone to church services this morning, Tess went upstairs to get her Bible.

Bobby glanced at her when she came into the room. "I can't stop thinking about Mitch," he admitted. "I wish I could have gone along with Declan."

Tess picked up her Bible and then turned to face her brother. "You can trust Declan. I'm sure he'll let us know what happened with Mitch."

"I wish I would have turned Mitch in to the police sooner," Bobby confessed. "If I had, he never would have been able to attack you."

"You can't think like that," she chided. "I've made a lot of mistakes, too, but all we can do is to learn from them and move forward."

"I guess you're right." Bobby waved a hand at her Bible. "I know I wasn't always good about going to church, but I prayed a lot after Mitch took off and left me alone. Going to church helped me cope. I was there twice before I stumbled across your note."

She smiled. "I'm glad to hear that. You need to believe that God is always there for you. I can read a few passages to you if you're interested."

He shrugged and then nodded. "Okay."

Tess sat on the edge of her bed and began to read from the book of Psalms. She expected her brother to lose interest, but he seemed to be paying close attention. In fact, they were so engrossed in the passages that she didn't realize until she'd finished that Declan was standing in the doorway listening in, as well.

"That was great," he said. "I always thought the Bible would be dull and boring."

"Tess knows how to make it interesting," Bobby said proudly, before changing the subject. "So, what happened with Mitch?"

Declan shrugged. "He didn't admit to assaulting Tess, but he's been arrested for possession with intent to sell. They were calling an ambulance to take him to the hospital when I left, because he seemed to be going through withdrawal."

"He's such an idiot," Bobby muttered, obviously disappointed that Mitch hadn't confessed. "You would have thought he'd stay away from drugs after seeing his mother drunk all the time, but maybe this will force him to get the help he needs."

"We'll pray for him," Declan said, surprising Tess. Did that mean he believed in God and the power of prayer? She was thrilled at how he'd listened to her reading from the Bible and hoped that he'd continue on this path, even after they'd gone their separate ways.

That thought was depressing, so she shook it off. "Praying for Mitch is a great idea." Tess took a deep breath and then bowed her head. "Dear

Lord, we ask that You heal Mitch Turner's addiction and show him the way to God. Amen."

"Amen," Bobby and Declan echoed simultaneously.

Tess smiled and felt a deep sense of contentment inside her. Being with Bobby and Declan together was nice, despite the fact that there was still a crazy bomber on the loose.

"Is there something we can do to help you find the guy who's after Tess?" Bobby asked as he crossed over to Declan.

He shrugged. "I wish there was. Maybe walking through the case again with the two of you will help."

"Sounds good to me," Bobby agreed.

"Go ahead, I'll be down in a little bit," Tess said.

Bobby and Declan clattered down to the first floor and she took a few minutes to include Declan and Bobby in her prayers.

Tess spent a few minutes in the bathroom, brushing her hair and putting on a coat of clear lip gloss before heading downstairs. She couldn't deny she wanted to look nice for Declan, and gave herself a mental scolding as she reached the living room.

She paused, listening to his deep voice as he talked to her brother. Her intent wasn't to eavesdrop, but when she heard Declan saying something about joining the marines, her temper flared.

"What were you telling Bobby?" she demanded as she marched into the kitchen. "I hope you weren't encouraging him to join the service."

"Calm down, sis. Declan was just telling me what worked for him, right? I didn't know he'd been in the marines."

Declan didn't say anything, and the warm, tender feelings she'd had toward him earlier quickly vanished.

"Bobby, we talked about this, remember?" Tess said, giving her brother an imploring look. "You said you'd be willing to give college a try. I get that joining the marines made sense for Declan, but you have other options. I have money set aside for your college tuition."

"I know I have options, Tess. There's no need to jump all over me."

She wanted to smack Declan for even putting the idea of joining the armed forces in Bobby's head in the first place. Why couldn't he leave well enough alone? Bobby was the only family she had left in the world, and the last thing she wanted to do was to risk losing him in some Third World country. Surely Declan wanted something better for his own kids?

She knew she was overreacting so she tried

to pull back her anger. "Don't do anything rash without talking to me, okay?" she said to Bobby. "Please?"

"I won't," Bobby promised.

She nodded, took a couple of deep, calming breaths and finally looked at Declan. "I thought you guys were going to review the case."

"We are. Have a seat…you can listen in, too."

Tess dropped into the chair closest to her brother. Declan cleared his throat and began reviewing the facts of the case.

"There have been a total of five bombs so far, the first one at the minimart, the second at the custard stand, the third beneath Tess's desk—"

"What?" Bobby interrupted. "I didn't know that the bomb was planted beneath Tess's desk. The only thing I heard was that it was at the elementary school."

Tess felt some of her anger melt away remembering how Declan saved her life just two days ago.

"There was a fourth bomb planted near your sister's car, too," Declan continued. "And the fifth one was found under the picnic table at Greenland Park. Each of these targets has a link to your sister."

"Don't forget, you're linked to some of those targets, as well," Tess said.

Declan nodded. "All of these sites are places

that kids tend to hang out, so that was one of the reasons that I thought someone like Mitch, or one of his buddies, may have had something to do with them."

Bobby shook his head. "Like I mentioned before, I never heard anything about this at school. If someone there is involved, they're not talking about it."

"Either way, I believe the bomber is someone local, or the targets would be different. They'd be bigger, like a baseball game, a festival, the theater or a music concert."

Tess's earlier contented mood evaporated. She knew that the rest of Declan's SWAT team were investigating the leads they had so far, but it seemed as if there was nothing more they could do, other than to wait for the bomber to make his next move.

Declan pushed restlessly away from the kitchen table. Talking through the case wasn't helping the way that he'd hoped, and he hated feeling helpless. Maybe he should be the one following Allan Gray. As far as he was concerned, the guy was at the top of his suspect list.

His phone rang and he was relieved to see that the caller was Caleb. "Hey, what's up?"

"I found out why Jeff Berg is on a leave of absence—his mother has been admitted to a local hospice, as she's apparently dying of cancer. I think we can take him off the list of suspects."

Declan let out a heavy sigh. "You're right. I guess that's a good reason to be on a leave of absence. Did Mitch say anything more before you shipped him off to the hospital?"

"Nah, he was babbling a bit and not making much sense. According to his doctor it'll be several days before we can talk to him again. And Isaac's team didn't find anything other than the usual drug paraphernalia at Mitchell's house, either."

Declan tried to look on the bright side, but it wasn't easy. "So the only real suspect we have left is Allan Gray."

"Don't forget the guy in the green ball cap, who may not be Allan Gray at all," Caleb said. "It's not like you to be so fixated on a suspect like Gray. Must be because he's Tess's neighbor."

"Point taken," Declan acknowledged, knowing he was letting his personal dislike of Gray get in the way of cool logic. It wasn't as if he had a reason to be jealous of Allan, not after the way Tess had shot daggers at him after she overheard his conversation with her brother. He knew she was mad, but she didn't realize Bobby had broached the subject first. Apparently her brother had already talked to an army recruiter, a small detail he obviously hadn't shared with Tess.

"I put the guy's basic description, as much as we could identify anyway, through the system to see if there are any other known bombers that might match it, but so far, nothing has popped." Declan knew that it was a long shot, since they didn't have an accurate height, weight or eye color to add.

"I can't think of anything more we can do," Caleb admitted. "I'm going home to spend time with my family. Let me know if you need anything."

"All right, thanks, Caleb." Declan disconnected from the call and glanced at Tess. "Jeff Berg's mother is dying of cancer, so that's why he's back in town."

"Poor Jeff," Tess murmured, her gaze full of sympathy.

Bobby grimaced. "I didn't like him much, but I feel bad for his mother."

"I was thinking," Tess said slowly. "We should go through our high school yearbooks. It's possible that seeing some of the photos of our classmates might jog our memories."

Declan lifted his eyebrows in surprise. "That's a great idea, Tess. I meant to do that earlier, especially because I want to get a look at Allan Gray. Give me a few minutes to go upstairs and dig them out."

He took the stairs two at a time, trying to

remember where he'd stored his stuff from high school. Had to be in one of the boxes he'd stashed in the back of his closet.

He should have thought of this sooner, even though it was probably a long shot. What were the chances that the bomber was someone they went to school with? Still, doing something was better than nothing.

He found the yearbooks, blowing the dust off before carrying them downstairs. As he set them on the kitchen table, his phone rang again. This time, the caller was Isaac.

"What's up?" Declan asked. "I thought you and Caleb were heading home to enjoy a day off."

"They called in another bomb, Deck. It's at the Greenland Grand Movie Theater."

A chill snaked down his spine as Isaac's words sank in. His sister, Karen, worked there. Was she working today? He didn't know, but if she was, this would be the second time she was in the path of a bomb. He strove to remain calm, even though his stomach was clenched with fear. "I'm on my way."

"What's wrong?" Tess asked.

"I have to go, another bomb has been found at the movie theater where my sister works." He didn't want to leave Tess and Bobby alone, but he didn't have a choice. His sister and other innocent lives were at stake. He grabbed his truck keys off the table. "You both need to stay here and keep hidden until you hear from me."

Tess's eyes were as large as saucers, but she nodded her agreement. "I'll pray for you."

"Be careful," Bobby added.

He gave a curt nod and rushed out to his truck, jamming the keys into the ignition and peeling out of his driveway, praying he'd get there in time.

*Please, Lord, keep my sister and everyone else at the movie theater safe from harm.*

# FIFTEEN

Tess watched Declan leave, feeling helpless. She couldn't imagine what he must be going through, knowing his sister's life could be in danger once again.

She closed her eyes and prayed for everyone's safety. When she opened her eyes, she was surprised and humbled to see that Bobby had been praying, as well.

Her brother flashed a sheepish grin. "Declan needs all the help he can get."

"I know." She didn't want to make a big deal out of it, so she gestured toward Declan's computer. "We can't sit here doing nothing—we need to figure out who is behind setting these bombs."

"We're not exactly trained investigators," Bobby reminded her. "But I agree that we need to try and do something to help. I still think Allan Gray could be involved." Bobby pulled Declan's computer around to face him. "Maybe Allan's on social media."

Tess reached for the yearbooks. "I'll start going through these. Maybe a picture of a younger version of Allan will spur a memory."

She opened the first book, which was Declan's freshman year. She would still have been in the middle school then, as she was a year younger. Once she found Declan's picture, she could hardly believe how young he looked. He wore his hair shorter then, but there was still a hard edge to his gaze, as if he'd already seen too much. She knew Declan had lived in the trailer park. Was being poor part of the reason he copped an attitude? Or was there more to the story?

She went back to find a picture of Allan Gray and winced at the photograph that was less than flattering. Poor Allan had suffered a bad case of acne and his hair looked unkempt. She stared at the picture for a long moment, vaguely remembering something about Allan having a sister. But was she older or younger?

Tess opened the other yearbooks, going through the *Grays,* searching for Allan's sister. She found a photograph of Alice Gray, who was a freshman during Declan's junior year. But there was no photograph of Alice in Declan's senior yearbook. Tess went back to the junior year and found a section in the back of the book where there was a list honoring the three students who had died that year. Two of them died in a terrible car crash, but the memorial for Alice only mentioned how she would be missed by all who knew her.

Tess sat back, remembering the incident now that she'd seen the memorial. Alice Gray had been found dead of a drug overdose. She'd taken a hodgepodge of pills from the family medicine cabinet. And if Tess remembered correctly, Allan had been the one to find his sister the following morning.

Was it possible that Allan somehow held Declan or the entire town responsible for his sister's suicide? Maybe this wasn't about Tess after all, but was actually all about Alice. Maybe Allan *was* savvy enough to set the bombs around the city.

As she went back to see Allan's picture she stumbled across a photograph of Steve Gains, the guy who'd attempted to assault her after the prom. Looking at him after all these years made her feel sick to her stomach. How could she have been so blind as to his true nature? Steve had been the star pitcher for the Greenland Gophers baseball team. He'd been offered a full scholarship to Arizona State University based on his talent. But she hadn't heard much about him after that; it was almost as if he'd dropped off the face of the earth.

She paged through the yearbook and found the group photograph of the entire baseball team. Their uniforms were white-and-green pin-striped pants with green jerseys and green baseball caps.

Abruptly she straightened in her seat, the tiny hairs on the back of her neck lifting in alarm. Steve Gains! Was it possible Steve was holding a grudge against Declan after all this time? It seemed ridiculous, yet she knew the person in the ball cap seemed familiar. The hair color and body type were the same. Steve Gains had to be the man in the green baseball cap that was captured on the video outside the school parking lot.

Maybe this wasn't about Alice Gray's suicide after all.

"Bobby, we need to find Declan's boss, Griff Vaughn, right away," she said, leaping to her feet in a rush.

"Why? What happened?"

"I think I found the bomber, and he has a good reason to hold a grudge against Declan. We need to hurry. It's possible they can find and arrest him outside the movie theater."

"Who?" Bobby asked skeptically.

"This guy here, Steve Gains." She tapped the photograph in the yearbook. "It's a long story that we don't have time to get into now. There isn't a moment to lose."

"Okay, but how are we going to get to the sheriff's department without a vehicle?" Bobby asked.

"Maybe we can take a taxi or something." Tess paced the small area of Declan's kitchen. "I don't think calling the guys from Declan's SWAT team will help, because they'll all be out at the movie theater."

"Just a minute." Bobby tapped on the keyboard of the laptop. "There's a bus stop a few blocks down the road. That will take us within a couple of blocks of the sheriff's department."

"Do you have a couple of bucks for the tickets?" she asked. "My cash is gone."

"Yeah, I have some money that Declan loaned to me."

Tess wondered why Declan had done that, but there wasn't time to get into it now. "Let's go." She didn't want to wait a second longer.

Tess led the way out through the side kitchen door, but she'd barely stepped outside when a large man holding a gun grabbed her roughly by the arm.

"Hi, Tess. Did you miss me over the past ten years?"

Her heart leaped into her throat as Steve Gains leered down at her, his eyes ice-cold with hatred. She wanted to shout at Bobby to run, but before she could move, Steve brought his hand down hard on her temple.

And for the third time in as many days, pain exploded in her head seconds before darkness claimed her.

Declan approached the ticket sales counter dressed in his full SWAT gear, beads of sweat trickling down his spine. Karen's eyes were wide with fear, but she sat completely still in her seat despite the bomb that was planted beneath the counter.

The setup was very similar to the one he'd rescued Tess from. Was it really just a few days ago? He couldn't afford to think about Tess and Bobby now. The first thing he'd done when he arrived was to send Isaac back over to his place to watch over them.

Just as Tess had done, Karen managed to activate the device when she sat down behind the ticket counter. He couldn't ignore the fact that there were four different ticket counters at the theater, which meant his sister had been targeted on purpose.

Tess was right: The bomber must be someone who hated Declan enough to target the people closest to him.

He smiled at his sister reassuringly. "Hang in

there, okay? I'm going to find a way to get you out of here."

Karen's smile was tremulous. "Declan, if anything happens to me I want you to take custody of Jenny and Josie."

"Nothing's going to happen," Declan promised. He didn't want to point out that if something happened to Karen, he'd likely die right alongside her. Because no matter what happened, he wasn't going to leave her here alone.

"I don't want Craig to get custody," Karen insisted. "He drinks and spanks them."

"Karen, I need you to calm down. We're going to beat this thing, okay? Now give me a few minutes to see what we're dealing with."

Karen didn't look pacified, but she didn't say anything more. Declan blew out a heavy sigh and knelt down on the floor, focusing his attention on the explosive device. It was almost an exact replica of the one that had been planted under Tess's desk, although he couldn't afford to assume the wiring inside was the same, as well.

In fact, he suspected the outside was made the same on purpose just so that he'd go down the same path in disarming the device.

He nudged Karen's seat out of the way as much as he dared, to make room to work. "It's the same perp," Declan said through his mic to Caleb.

"Roger, Deck. Can you disarm it?"

"Affirmative." He injected confidence in his tone to reassure his sister more than anything.

He found himself praying as he quickly identified and removed the dummy wires. *Please, Lord, guide me on the right path to saving my sister and other innocent lives today. I need Your strength and courage to assist me. Please show me the way!*

Soon Declan was down to the three wires that consisted of the timer, the trigger and the ground.

For a moment panic seized him. What if he made a mistake? Jenny and Josie would be motherless and whoever had set this bomb would eventually find Tess and Bobby. And the deaths wouldn't stop there. For all he knew the perp would move on to even bigger targets. He couldn't bear the thought of having so many lives resting on his shoulders.

"Deck, is everything okay?" Caleb asked through his headset.

"Yeah, two minutes and counting." Declan swiped his hands down the sides of his pants, trying to rein in his turbulent emotions. Failure was not an option. And he wasn't alone; God was with him.

A sense of peace washed over him, despite the timer that continued to count down ominously.

He really did believe that God was guiding him and knew he had to trust his instincts. By now, he knew exactly what the bomber was thinking when he created these devices. He could almost sense what had gone through the perp's mind.

Declan lifted the wire cutters and clipped the wire located between the timer and the end of the device. Instantly the clock went dark.

"I think I have it," he muttered. Two wires were left and he held his breath as he clipped the second wire that was closest to the timer.

Nothing happened. No explosion. No boom. He'd managed to successfully disarm the device.

"Move your knee away from the side of the device," Declan instructed.

"Are you sure?" Karen asked anxiously.

"I'm sure."

Karen slowly eased her knee away from the trigger.

"Now slide your chair away from the counter," Declan told his sister. "Easy, now."

Karen whimpered a bit but did as he instructed, pushing her wheeled chair away from the counter. When she was far enough away, she rose shakily to her feet. "Thank you, Declan. I was so afraid I'd end up in the hospital again, or worse."

He got to his feet and wrapped his arms

around her in a big hug. "You're welcome. Now go home and hug your girls for me."

"I won't forget this," she whispered.

"I know," he murmured. He cleared his throat and stepped back, clicking on his mic. "Caleb, I'm sending my sister out now. The device has been disarmed, but we need to get this thing into a reinforced box as soon as possible."

"Roger, Deck. Good job," Caleb responded. "As soon as your sister is clear, I'll bring in the box."

"Have you heard from Isaac?"

"Negative, but I'll check in with him soon. Right now we have to focus on the device."

Declan suppressed a flash of irritation. He knew the bomb was important, but he thought it was odd that he hadn't heard from Isaac. Surely his buddy would have at least checked in to say everything was okay?

He knelt back down to figure out the best way to get the bomb detached from the underside of the ticket counter. This wouldn't be as easy as cutting through a metal school desk. The counter was roughly two inches thick. How did the perp get the bomb attached anyway?

"Deck, are you there?" Caleb asked.

"Affirmative, what's up?"

"Isaac is at your place, but Tess and Bobby aren't there."

"What?" he asked sharply. "What do you mean? They have to be there. Make sure he checks the entire house, including the basement."

"Isaac has confirmed the house is empty, including the basement," Caleb said in a calm tone. "Do you have any idea where they might be?"

"No, I told them to stay there until they heard from me. Are there signs of a struggle?"

"Negative. Deck, why don't you come out here? I'll take over inside."

Declan didn't have to be told twice. The bomb might have been neutralized for the moment, but it was still dangerous. He could hear his boss arguing through his headset, demanding Declan stay to finish the job.

But Declan pulled off his headset, refusing to listen. Griff could fire him if he wanted, but no way was he going to sit here while Tess and Bobby were missing.

He could only pray that nothing bad had happened to them.

Declan pulled into his driveway behind Isaac's truck. Isaac came out to meet him. "They might have left on their own, Deck."

He didn't want to believe it, although he'd already tried calling and texting without a response. "Are you absolutely sure that there's no sign of foul play?"

Isaac spread his hands wide. "Not that I could tell. Take a look for yourself."

Declan brushed past his teammate to go inside. The first thing he noticed was the yearbooks spread out across the table. The books were closed, but he wondered if maybe Tess had been looking through them for clues. Had she found something incriminating against Allan Gray?

He swept a glance over the room. Nothing else seemed to be out of place. However, the kitchen chairs had been pushed in, which struck him as odd. If Tess and Bobby had left in a hurry, would they have bothered to make sure the chairs were neatly tucked against the table?

The laptop computer was closed, and he lifted the screen and pushed the start button to bring it to life. There were two different search tabs open, one for local bus routes and another for a popular social media website, but he couldn't tell if Bobby had found anything of importance.

"I don't like it," he muttered darkly. "Why on earth would they leave? And on a bus? To where?"

"Maybe they were trying to get out to the movie theater," Isaac suggested. "Could be they stumbled upon some sort of clue."

"Call Caleb, see if they showed up there after I left." Declan pulled one of the yearbooks closer, half listening as Isaac made the call. He opened it up, searching for a picture of Allan Gray.

The image didn't spark any memories and he battled a wave of helplessness. He didn't have time to sit here trying to retrace the steps Tess and Bobby had taken. He needed to know they were safe.

"No sign of them at the movie theater," Isaac confirmed. "Griff's not too happy with you, either."

Declan shrugged. "I did my part, Caleb, and the rest of the team can get the device out of there."

Isaac blew out a heavy sigh. "Look, Deck, there's nothing more we can do here. I'm sure Tess will get in touch with you soon."

Declan shook his head. "I can't let it go. Something's just not right. The kitchen chairs are neat, but the yearbooks are spread all over. Was the door locked when you arrived?"

"No," Isaac admitted. "But if they left in a hurry, they may have forgotten to lock the door behind them."

Declan walked back over toward the door and peered along the door frame. It took a few minutes for him to find the crimson stain. "Does this look like blood?" he asked hoarsely.

Isaac came over and rubbed his finger across the stain. "Maybe."

"They didn't leave of their own accord, I'm sure of it." Declan spun around and went back to the yearbooks. If they had in fact been taken by force, surely they would have tried to leave some sort of clue behind.

"What are you looking for?" Isaac asked.

"I don't know, but hopefully I'll figure it out when I see it."

Isaac joined him in searching through the yearbooks. "Hey, Deck, check this out."

"What?" Declan glanced over at the yearbook Isaac had open.

"This page was bent over. Do you think either Tess or Bobby left it like this on purpose?"

Declan peered at the page, realizing that the point of the page was right next to a photograph of Steve Gains.

Gains? The guy who'd tried to assault Tess on prom night? Suddenly everything made sense and he mentally kicked himself for not considering the possibility sooner.

This creep would be crazy enough to carry a grudge against him, and using Tess to get to him would be the icing on the cake. Poetic justice, at least in Steve's mind.

"Steve Gains has Tess and Bobby," he said in a choked voice. "And I think he's the bomber, too. We have to find him, before it's too late!"

# SIXTEEN

"Tess? Wake up, sis. I need you to wake up!"

The urgency in Bobby's voice cut through the fog that seemed to have shrouded her mind. Tess blinked and lifted her head, wincing at the pain in her neck and temple as she tried to peer through the dim light. "Bobby?"

"Thank God you're all right." The anguish in his tone made her think she must have been unconscious for a long time.

It took a few minutes for her to realize that she was sitting in a chair with her arms bound behind her back with something that felt sticky, like duct tape. Bobby was sitting across from her, no doubt tied up in a similar manner. Her shoulders ached from the stress of her arms being wrenched behind her, but the pain was not nearly as bad as the throbbing in her head.

She probably had another concussion, on top of the one she already had. She was really annoyed at the way these losers kept hitting her in the head.

"Where are we?" she asked in a whisper.

"Some cabin in the woods," Bobby murmured. "I'm sorry, Tess. He held a gun on you, so I didn't dare try to get away. I didn't want to risk your life."

"It's okay, Bobby," she assured him, even though she secretly wished her brother had saved himself. Unfortunately, there wasn't anything she could do about it now. Maybe together they could find a way out of here.

She struggled against the duct tape tying her wrists together, biting back a cry as pain reverberated up her arms. Was duct tape really that strong? Or had Steve used something else first and then added the duct tape as a precautionary measure?

"Is Tess finally awake?" Steve Gains's harsh voice echoed through the sparsely furnished cabin.

Tess turned her head toward Steve's voice, swallowing hard when she noticed he had a box-like device along with several other items spread out on the rough-hewn table across the room. Her heart sank as the implication hit home.

Steve was planning to build another bomb. And she had no doubt this time he intended to kill her and Bobby. She hated to admit that

Steve's timing was perfect. He must have purposefully set the bomb at the movie theater to keep Declan busy saving his sister, clearing the way for him to come after her and Bobby. And even once Declan managed to defuse the bomb at the movie theater, there was no way he could know where she and Bobby were being held. Steve wasn't even one of Declan's top suspects.

Her stomach clenched with nausea. They were on their own.

"I don't understand what's going on, Steve," Tess said, trying to placate the man who clearly held a grudge for all these years. "Why are you doing this?"

"You just don't get it, do you?" he asked sharply. "My life is over and it's your fault! And Shaw's, too!"

Tess fought to control her instinctive reaction to his absurd allegation. Why on earth would anything that happened to Steve Gains be her fault? He was the one who tried to assault her, not the other way around.

"Obviously you've been setting these bombs around the city, but I still don't understand why," she said. "It's not as if the innocent people you've involved are responsible for what happened to you."

"This town turned its back on me a long time ago," Steve said, sneering. "I was kicked out of college, did you know that? And then a couple of those snotty sorority chicks accused me of raping them, so I was arrested and thrown in jail. Do you have any idea what it's like inside the joint? Do you have any clue what I've been through?" His voice and facial expression reflected the depth of his desperation, and for a moment she felt bad for him. "And then just a few months before my release, I see a picture of Declan and some other cop being called heroes because they saved some kid. Well, I've shown him."

"I'm sorry, Steve. But now that you're home, I'm sure things will get better."

"Liar!" he shouted, a wild look in his eyes. Tess swallowed hard, wondering if he was going to lose it and simply kill them outright. "Being here is even worse! I've been turned down for every job I applied for! The minute they found out about my prison record, I wasn't worthy enough to wipe the mud off their shoes. Well, now they'll be sorry for the way they treated me. I'll show them who's in charge around here. And it's not Shaw!"

Tess glanced helplessly at Bobby, wishing there was some way to get through to Steve. But how? Apparently he was too far gone to listen to reason. Somehow he'd rationalized that all the failures in his life were because of her and Declan. She swallowed hard, knowing her initial instincts were right. Declan was the real target. No doubt, Steve planned to use her and Bobby as bait.

And she didn't want to think that this time Steve might succeed in building a bomb Declan couldn't defuse.

"Declan will find us," Bobby spoke up confidently. "He's smart and you won't be showing the people around here anything except how pathetic you are once you're back in jail. If you were smart, you'd leave now while you have a head start, because if you wait much longer it'll be too late."

"I'm not going back to jail!" Steve shouted. And for a moment his eyes narrowed thoughtfully as if he was seriously considering his options. Had her brother's harsh words penetrated Steve's irrational obsession? Was he thinking of taking Bobby's advice and leaving them alone?

But no, Steve abruptly turned back to the items he had strewn across the table, clearly intending to create the bomb as soon as possible.

Tess closed her eyes against a wave of despair.

*Please, Lord, help Declan get here in time. Please keep me and Bobby safe in Your care. We ask for Your grace and mercy, in this desperate time. Amen.*

* * *

Declan scrubbed his hands over his face, battling duel waves of fear and worry. He had to find out where Steve had taken Tess and Bobby. But so far his internet searches hadn't come up with any clues.

"We need to call the feds," he said, looking over at Isaac. "They have better resources than we do."

"All right, keep searching while I make the call."

Since no addresses had popped up under Steve's name, Declan tried to find his parents. But he didn't have a clue as to what their first names were, and there were more than one Gains in the online white pages listing.

"We may have to go to each place ourselves," Declan muttered as he listened to Isaac's one-sided conversation with the FBI. He jotted down the addresses that were closest to Greenland High School, although truthfully, Steve's parents could have moved at any point in the past ten years.

"Agent Piermont is going to get back to us," Isaac said after he'd disconnected from the call.

"So she believes me about Steve Gains being the bomber?" Declan asked.

Isaac grimaced. "I wouldn't go that far. She

thinks your theory is far-fetched but agreed it was a lead worth following up."

Declan sighed and continued working on his list. "We have three addresses here for the last name Gains. We don't have time to sit around waiting for the feds to get back to us. We need to start checking these places out now."

Isaac hesitated and then slowly nodded. "Okay, should we split up? Caleb and the rest of the team are still working with getting the device out of the theater, but we can ask Griff to free up a couple of the guys."

Declan shook his head. "I don't think so. The boss isn't too happy with me at the moment. Let's wait to see what the feds come up with first. For now we'll split up. You take this address here and I'll take this one." Declan tore the sheet of paper he had into two parts before handing the lower half to Isaac.

"Keep in touch," Isaac said as they strode outside.

"I will. And let me know as soon as you hear from the feds," Declan said.

"Will do."

Declan punched the first address on his list into the map application on his phone. Driving to the small house that was located in a nice but older neighborhood didn't take too long, and he was encouraged when he saw there was a car sitting in the driveway. At least someone was home.

Still dressed in his SWAT gear, Declan approached the front door of the Gains household. He hoped his official attire would help elicit the cooperation of the occupants inside. He knocked and waited impatiently for someone to answer the door.

The seconds stretched into a full minute before the door opened a crack. "Yes?" a frail voice asked. "What do you want?"

Declan smiled at the elderly woman who answered the door. "I'm sorry to bother you, ma'am, but I'm looking for Steve Gains. Are you his grandmother?"

"Eh?" The elderly woman leaned closer to the door while still hanging on to the frame for support.

"I'm looking for Steve Gains," Declan repeated in a louder tone. "Does he live here with you?"

"Stevie? No, he doesn't live here." The woman wrinkled her brow. "I think he's still in Arizona."

There was no point in arguing with the poor woman; it was clear she hadn't seen Steve anytime recently. "Where do Steve's parents live? Do you know their address?"

"His father still lives on Elmwood Parkway,

but I don't think he's home. George? *George!* Has Ronnie come back from California?"

Declan winced as she shouted to her husband. He glanced down at the slip of paper in his hand. The third address on his list was on Elmwood Boulevard, not parkway but close enough.

"That's okay, thanks for your help," Declan said as he turned away. He jogged back to his car, grabbing his ringing phone as he slid into the seat. "Steve's father lives at 1107 Elmwood Boulevard," he said to Isaac.

"You work fast. Agent Piermont just called to confirm that, as well. But she also told me that Steve spent the past seven years in jail, so now they believe he could be the bomber."

Declan felt a surge of satisfaction, but knowing that Steve was the guy behind it all was one thing. Getting to him before he hurt Bobby and Tess was something else.

"Steve's father has a fishing cabin located about forty minutes away near Percy Lake," Isaac continued. "The address is 659 Range Road."

Forty minutes? He didn't like the sound of that. "Steve could be at his father's house, too, since it sounds like he's not home. Why don't you go over to the parents' place in case Steve is there and I'll head up to the cabin on Percy Lake?"

"You should have backup with you. Do you want me to call the feds?" Isaac asked.

"Yeah, we need all the help we can get. I'll let you know as soon as I reach the cabin. If you find Steve before me, let me know."

"Roger that. Be careful, Deck."

"You, too." Declan disconnected from the call and quickly programmed the new address into the GPS application on his phone. Twisting the key in the ignition, he flipped on the red lights on the top of his vehicle and then gunned the engine, backing quickly out of the driveway.

He needed to get to the cabin in less time than forty minutes. And he hoped and prayed that Tess and Bobby could hang on long enough.

Tess glanced nervously at Steve as Bobby inched his chair closer to hers. How much time did they have before Steve finished his bomb? She had no way of knowing for sure.

Bobby groaned under his breath as he struggled against the bonds that held his wrists together. If he was tied as tightly as she was, he would only end up hurting himself.

"Be careful," she murmured in a low tone. "He'll hear you."

Bobby shook his head and continued to fight the duct-taped rope that Steve had used to tie them up. She tried to do the same, but the pain radiating through her head and shoulders made it impossible.

She dropped her chin to her chest, fighting a strong sense of hopelessness. The odds were overwhelmingly stacked against them. She'd prayed over and over again, but still Steve continued working on the bomb he was creating and she knew it was a matter of minutes, not hours, before he'd put his destructive plan into place.

"Come on, Tess. Don't give up," Bobby coaxed. "We're not beat yet."

She looked up at her brother, struck by the way Bobby had matured over the past few days. In the face of adversity, he'd grown into a confident young man, a far cry from the troubled teen she'd worried and prayed about.

Tears pricked her eyes at the thought that he might not live to graduate from high school, attend college, fall in love or get married.

She pulled herself up short. *Enough wallowing in self-pity, already!* Bobby was right—they weren't beaten yet. In fact, the way he was moving his left arm indicated he might be close to getting loose.

"I left Declan a clue about Steve," her brother confessed in a low tone. "We have to believe he'll get here in time."

"Really?" Tess didn't try to hide the admiration in her tone. "Very smart, Bobby. I'm proud of you."

Her brother flushed and ducked his head as if embarrassed. "I'm sorry for everything I've done over the past few years, Tess. I know I wasn't the easiest person to live with. But I promise that once we're out of here, I'll make it up to you."

Tears threatened again. "I love you, Bobby. No matter what happens, you need to remember that."

"Right back at you, sis."

Praying in earnest, she watched as Bobby continued to work against the restraints holding his wrists together. She wasn't sure what they could possibly do against Steve Gains, who was armed not only with a gun but with the bomb he was making.

But there was a chance that with the right set of circumstances, Bobby could catch Steve off guard. All they needed was a little luck and a lot of faith.

Declan slowed his speed and shut off the red and blue lights as he approached Ranger Road. He made the trip in less than twenty minutes, and Isaac had already called him to let him know that there was no one at Steve's parents' house.

He knew he'd find Gains at the cabin, hopefully along with Bobby and Tess. What better place to build bombs than out in the middle of an isolated cabin on a lake?

When the GPS on his phone indicated he was two-tenths of a mile away from the cabin, he pulled off onto the shoulder and shut down the engine. He set his phone to vibrate and tucked it in his pocket before climbing out of the car. Reaching into the backseat, he grabbed his M4 .223 sniper rifle and his Glock. He took the time to load them before closing the door softly and heading off on foot.

Declan wanted to get to the cabin as quickly as possible, but he couldn't afford to let Steve see him, either. Thankfully the area around the cabin was full of trees and brush, so he set off on an angled path from the road in the same general direction that the cabin was located.

He walked slowly, peering through the brush for the cabin. Had he gone past it by accident? No, there it was, a log cabin nicely camouflaged behind the trees with its brown logs and green trim.

The cabin was about a hundred yards away, but he was hesitant to go any closer. Slinging his M4 over his shoulder, he climbed a nearby tree for a better position.

Declan was sweating by the time he settled in the branches of the large tree. It was early enough in September that there were plenty of leaves clinging to the branches, which provided decent cover, but they also blocked his view. Moving carefully, he pulled his M4 off his shoulder and brought the business end up so that he could peer through the scope. It took him a few seconds to pinpoint the cabin, and his breath lodged in his throat when he saw a man with his head bent down, working on something that was on the table.

The guy had to be Steve Gains. And a sick sense of urgency hit as Declan realized Gains was building another bomb.

Where were Bobby and Tess? The window along the front of the cabin was wide, and he carefully tracked along the bottom edge until he caught a glimpse of two figures seated in chairs on the other side of the room.

Bobby and Tess! They were still alive, although clearly bound to their respective seats.

His phone vibrated with an incoming call, and he braced himself in position prior to answering it. "Yeah?"

"Is Steve there?" Isaac asked.

"Affirmative. He's building a bomb and he has Bobby and Tess, too."

"The feds are on their way and so am I," Isaac informed him. "ETA is less than fifteen minutes."

Fifteen minutes was an eternity if Steve was

anywhere close to finishing the bomb. "Okay, but I can't guarantee I'll wait if Gains makes a move. Get here as soon as you can."

"Understood."

Declan disconnected from the call and put his phone back in his pocket. He lifted the M4 again and found a niche in the tree branches to help steady it. He didn't want to think about the fact that he wasn't the best sharpshooter on the SWAT team. Granted, he'd been working hard to improve, but everyone knew that his area of expertise was defusing bombs, not hitting the center of a target at a hundred and fifty yards.

Sweat trickled down the sides of his face as he watched Steve Gains through the scope. The man abruptly stood, a sinister smirk spread across his face. He turned and said something to Bobby and Tess. Was he telling them the bomb was finished? Was he taunting them with his plan of killing them?

Declan tightened his grip on the M4, knowing that if the bomb was in fact finished, there wasn't a moment to lose. Right now he had the element of surprise on his side. If he waited too long, Gains could move away from the window and his opportunity to take him out would be gone.

Declan drew in a deep breath, knowing he had to shoot twice, once to break the window and then a second time to hit his target. He adjusted his aim for the trajectory of the bullet and slowly pulled the trigger.

The M4's retort pierced the air as the window of the cabin shattered. He took his second shot a millisecond later and then stared through the scope, desperately looking for Steve. Had he missed? Dear Lord above, he couldn't have missed!

There was no sign of Gains. Declan didn't dare believe he'd actually hit his target.

"Help us!" a female voice shouted. Tess? He moved the scope and saw that Bobby had thrown himself across Tess in an attempt to protect his sister.

"I'm coming!" Declan shouted. He swung the M4 back over his shoulder and quickly descended from the tree. "Where's Gains?"

"He's hit! Hurry!"

Declan swung down to the ground and took off running toward the cabin. He pulled his Glock and flattened himself against the side wall next to the door. He twisted the knob and shoved the door open while keeping out of sight.

"Look out, he has a gun!"

Everything happened so fast it was nothing more than a blur. He tucked and rolled through the doorway, in the direction where he estimated Tess and Bobby were located. A gunshot echoed through the cabin and he quickly brought up his Glock and aimed again at Steve Gains who was lying on the floor drenched in blood.

He shot Gains a second time and the man finally fell back, his gun dropping uselessly to the floor. Declan quickly ran over to retrieve Gains's gun, checked for a pulse, not surprised that it wasn't there before looking over at Tess and Bobby, relieved when he didn't see any blood.

"Are you both okay?" he asked as he came over to help straighten Bobby's chair so that he was off Tess.

"We are now," Tess said in a wobbly voice. "Thank heavens you made it in time."

"The power of prayer," Declan murmured as he dug in his pocket for a knife to cut them both loose.

The danger was over. Tess and Bobby were safe. The sounds of sirens indicated his backup would be here shortly.

*Thank You, Lord!*

# SEVENTEEN

Tess bit back a cry of pain when Declan cut through the binds holding her hands behind her back. Red spots danced in front of her eyes as her arms fell uselessly to her sides. For several long moments she waited for the pain to recede and the blood to circulate normally before she could move. She watched as he freed Bobby, as well.

"Tess? Are you sure you're okay?" Declan asked, coming back over to help her stand.

She swayed and Declan hauled her close. Gratefully, she leaned against him, absorbing his strength. "I'm just so glad you made it here in time," she murmured.

"Me, too," Declan admitted, resting his cheek on her hair. "I was worried sick that I'd be too late."

"Steve was going to kill all of us," she confided. "He blamed you and me for everything that went wrong in his life."

"He won't hurt anyone ever again," Declan promised.

There was a commotion from outside and Tess glanced up to see Bobby heading over to the doorway. "Hey, it looks like the rest of your team is here," Bobby said.

Tess caught Declan's gaze. "I guess you should go out and fill them in," she said, stepping back to move out of his embrace.

"Tess…" Declan's voice trailed off as he cupped her cheek in his palm. "There's so much I want to tell you."

She smiled gently. "I have some things I'd like to tell you, too, but let's finish this up first, okay? We can talk more later."

He surprised her by giving her a quick, tender kiss, before releasing her. Her heart raced and she had to take a deep breath to calm herself before she crossed over to stand next to Bobby. She glanced at Steve Gains's body lying in front of the table covered in blood, and then quickly averted her gaze.

"Good job, Deck," Isaac said as he crossed over to kneel beside Steve.

"Not really, I didn't want to kill him. Now we'll never know exactly what was going on in his head."

"You may still get that chance to talk to him, because I'm pretty sure he still has a pulse."

Isaac glanced up. "Get the ambulance crew in here, now!"

"What? I checked for a pulse," Declan protested.

"Maybe it stopped momentarily from shock," Isaac said.

Tess and Bobby stepped back out of the way so the ambulance crew could get to Steve. The two paramedics quickly went to work, one starting an IV and hanging fluids while the other one applied pressure to the gunshot wound.

"I hope he makes it," Declan muttered. "I'd really like to know his true motive."

"I can tell you what he told us about why he was doing this," she offered. "He ranted a lot before he finished working on the bomb."

"We'll take over the interviews from here," a woman said, stepping forward. She was dressed in a navy blue suit, her long dark hair pulled back severely from her face, and it took Tess a moment to realize she was one of the FBI agents Declan had mentioned.

Declan and Isaac glanced at each other, and Tess could tell they weren't happy about the feds interfering with the case.

"Please come with me," the FBI agent said.

She shot Declan a helpless glance, before reluctantly following the female agent outside to the clearing around the cabin.

"I'm coming, too," Bobby said loyally.

The agent stopped several feet away from the front door of the cabin and began to rattle off a series of questions. Together Tess and Bobby relayed their account about how Steve had accosted them at Declan's house and brought them here. Agent Piermont kept interrupting them, so it took far longer than it should have to get through all the details.

"Apparently Steve's father had a criminal record for sexual assault, too," Agent Piermont informed them.

"Did I hear you right?" Declan asked as he came over. "Steve's father also served time for sexual assault?"

"Yes, although it was a long time ago," Agent Piermont admitted. "His mother left when Steve was five years old, leaving his father to raise the boy alone. I have to wonder if the son learned a little too much from his father."

Declan paled and nodded, turning abruptly away. Tess frowned and started to follow him, but just then the ambulance crew came outside rolling Gains on the gurney.

Within moments, the ambulance whisked the perp away to meet up with the Flight For Life helicopter that was landing somewhere close by. The roar of the chopper blades made it difficult to hear anything that was going on. When Tess turned back to find Declan, she noticed he was talking to his boss, the two men wearing matching solemn expressions on their faces.

Tess sucked in a quick breath as Declan handed over his handgun and a rifle to his boss, before turning away and crossing over to meet them.

"What happened?" she asked. "Are you in trouble?"

"Normal operating procedure in a police shooting," he said, waving off her concern. "I've been cleared to head home since I'm officially on administrative duty."

Tess didn't like the sound of that. "What is wrong with your boss? Doesn't he realize you saved our lives? If you hadn't shot Steve, who knows what would have happened? This lunatic was getting ready to plant the bomb between me and Bobby."

"Hey, it's okay, Tess. They have to investigate no matter what," he said softly. "You already gave your statement to the feds so Griff and the rest of the brass will eventually find out that the shooting was justified. It'll just take some time to get through all the forensics that will support my case."

"I still don't like it," she muttered. "They should know you well enough to realize you wouldn't shoot unless you had no choice."

"Come on, let's go home." Declan held out his hand and she gladly took it, ignoring Bobby's smirk.

The ride back to Declan's house was relatively quiet, and Tess gratefully leaned back and closed her eyes, willing her splitting headache to go away. She hadn't mentioned it to Declan, because she knew he'd make her go back to the hospital to be checked out, and she already knew from her first visit that there wasn't much they could do about her concussion anyway.

"Are you sure you're okay?" Declan asked.

"Just tired and sore, that's all."

"She needs to rest," Bobby spoke up from the backseat. "She's been through a lot."

Tess must have dozed, because it seemed like barely five minutes later that Declan was pulling into his driveway. She knew she should insist on going home, but she didn't have the energy to argue with him. Before she could move, Declan had come around to open the passenger door.

"Come on, let's get you upstairs to get some sleep," he said.

"I can walk," she muttered.

Declan ignored her protest and wrapped his arm around her waist to assist her as Bobby went ahead and opened the doors. Declan helped her upstairs to the second-floor bedroom that she'd been sharing with Bobby.

Once she reached the bedroom she gratefully sank into the bed, barely noticing that Declan left her alone, softly closing the door behind him.

When Tess woke up again, the room was dim and through the window she could see the sun was low on the horizon. Gingerly sitting up at the side of the bed, she was grateful to note that the throbbing in her head had faded to nothing more than a very minor ache. After freshening up in the bathroom, she made her way downstairs. She could hear voices outside and had to smile when she realized Declan and Bobby were outside grilling dinner.

She opened the door and then froze, when she heard their conversation.

"Tess doesn't know about my meeting with the army recruiter," her brother was saying.

"You need to talk to her, Bobby. You know she cares about you."

"But she doesn't want to hear my side of it," her brother argued.

"You still need to discuss this with her."

"Yes, you do need to talk to me," Tess said as she opened the door and stepped outside. She shot Declan a narrow glare. "I thought I asked you to stop encouraging him to join the service."

Declan lifted his eyebrows. "I didn't encourage him, Tess. Go ahead and ask your brother when he went to visit the recruiter. He'll tell you that it was well before any of this happened."

Tess didn't want to believe it, but she knew Declan was probably right. Bobby and Declan had only been together for the past two days, and there had been no time to visit a recruiter considering all the events that had taken place in the past forty-eight hours. Still, this was the second time she'd overheard Declan and Bobby talking about the armed forces, and as far as she was concerned, that was two times too many.

"Well?" she asked, looking at her brother.

Bobby ducked his head and shuffled his feet. "Mitch and I visited with the recruiter the first time in April. But then Mitch started using drugs, so I went to see the recruiter again by myself right before school started."

Tess's heart sank at her brother's words. "I thought we had this conversation, Bobby. I thought you agreed that you'd give college a try."

Bobby shrugged. "I know that's what you want me to do, Tess, but I'm not sure college is the right choice for me. And look at Declan. He went from the marines to being a cop! Joining the service worked out fine for him."

Tess was so angry she could barely think straight. "Declan's situation is different."

"No, it's not…you just don't understand."

Tess didn't want to have this conversation

here. Clearly she and her brother needed to have a heart-to-heart conversation, alone. "I'd like to go home, Declan. Now."

"Come on, sis, you're overreacting."

Tess folded her hands over her chest. "Either you agree to take us home, or I'll call Caleb or Isaac for a ride. Your choice."

"I'll take you," Declan agreed in a subdued tone. "Just let me take the burgers and brats off the fire so they don't burn."

"I was looking forward to eating them, too," her brother muttered loud enough so she could hear. "It's been hours since breakfast."

Tess turned away, feeling helpless. She couldn't bring herself to ignore her brother's need to eat dinner. He'd been through a lot today, too. "Fine, we can eat first and then go home." Without waiting for a response, she went back inside and shut the door behind her. Fighting tears, she sat down at the kitchen table and held her head in her hands.

She didn't want to lose her brother to the army. And if Declan cared about her at all, he wouldn't encourage her brother to join the service.

Which only made her realize that Declan might not feel the same way she did.

The moment he'd burst through Steve's cabin door to save them, she realized how much she loved him. She always had a soft spot for him back when she was in high school, but they'd gone their separate ways. Being with him these past few days made her realize she loved the man he'd become. And up until now, she'd also loved the way he'd been such an awesome role model for her brother.

But that was before all this. If her brother joined the army, she'd never forgive him.

Apparently she'd have to find a way to move on with her life, without Declan.

Declan flipped the brats and burgers, wondering if he'd blown his chance with Tess after the way she demanded to be taken home.

"Don't worry about my sister," Bobby told him. "She'll get over being mad at you. One thing about Tess, she can't hold a grudge for very long."

Declan wasn't too sure about that. He stared blindly down at the grill. Had Bobby taken his willingness to talk about the service as encouragement? That hadn't been his intention. Joining the marines had worked for him, but then again, his home life had been very different.

"I'll go talk to her," Bobby offered, obviously anxious to make amends. "I'll make sure she knows this is my decision and not yours."

Declan watched as Bobby disappeared back inside the house. When the brats and burgers were cooked to his satisfaction, he removed them from the grill and piled them on a platter. He carried it inside. Tess and Bobby were seated next to each other and he winced when he saw that Tess had been crying.

He set the platter down on the counter and turned to face them. "Look, Bobby, there's something you need to know before you make this decision. I did join the marines, but at the time I was mainly trying to escape my father." A muscle twitched in his cheek. "You see, my old man was a mean drunk. My mother left him and took my sister with her, and my dad used to smack me around until I was old enough to defend myself."

"Wow...that must have been rough," Bobby said sympathetically.

"It was. Maybe if my mom had stuck around, things would have been different. So I'm going to be honest with you here—if I'd had the same support system you have with Tess, I'm not so sure I would have enlisted."

"But you said that it was an honor to serve our country," Bobby protested.

He couldn't bear Tess's accusing gaze. "Yes, it is an honor to serve our country. But you also need to understand just how many men and women have died for their country. My best friend, Tony, was standing right next to me when he was shot and killed."

He heard Tess gasp in horror, and as much as he wanted to stop, he knew it would be best if they knew the truth about everything.

"When my tour was up, I lost control of my life," Declan continued. "Tony's death had been difficult to deal with. He had a wife and a son. Why was he the one to die that day? I kept thinking it should have been me."

"Oh, Declan," Tess cried. "That must have been awful, but you know that it's not up to us to question God's plan."

He shrugged. "I didn't have faith back then. I spent months trying to drown my grief in the bottom of a whiskey bottle. And when my sister came to find me, I lashed out at her in anger. Thankfully I didn't hurt her, but it was then that I realized that I'd become my father." Baring his soul like this wasn't easy, but he owed it to Tess to convince her brother that he had other options. "Bobby, you have your sister's faith, love and support. Just make sure you're joining the army for the right reasons, and not as a way to escape."

"Man, I'm sorry to hear about your friend," Bobby murmured in shock.

"Tony was a good man, and there are still days

I think that it should have been me who died instead of him."

Tess surprised him by jumping out of her seat and coming over to wrap her arms around his waist. "Declan, I'm sorry for everything you've had to go through. I'm sure your sister understood that you were in pain, hurting over the death of your friend."

He couldn't stop himself from hugging her back. "Thanks, but that's no excuse. I sobered up and decided then and there that I wouldn't drink again. I attended the police academy and graduated at the top of my class. But it wasn't easy to move on." He swallowed hard. "When I heard that Steve's father had a history of sexual assaults, it reminded me that my father's blood runs in my veins, too. Don't you see how similar we are? Steve's mother abandoned him, too."

"Declan, don't you dare compare yourself to Steve. And you're not your father, either. I could see the goodness in you the night you rescued me from Steve's assault. I'm sorry that your father hurt you, but can't you see how different you are from him?" Drawing a breath, she continued softly. "You've made the decision to make something of yourself, to serve our country and to give back to your community. You've learned about faith and have accepted God's calling. I'm proud of the man you've become."

His throat closed with emotion and he pulled her close, hoping and praying that Tess would be willing to take a chance on him. "Thanks," he managed. "Does this mean you'll give me the opportunity to prove how much I care about you?"

Tess tipped her head back to smile up at him. "Of course, Declan. Because I care about you, too."

The timing wasn't perfect, but Declan decided that if he was going to bare his soul, he might as well go all the way. "Good to know, because I love you, Tess. For years I told myself that I didn't want a family, but that was just an excuse to avoid relationships. When I realized Steve had you, I knew how much I loved you. And I hope and pray that someday you'll learn to love me, too."

Tess smiled, her eyes filling with tears. "You don't have to wait, Declan. I love you. I love you very much."

"I'm glad," he whispered before capturing her mouth in a deep, heart-stirring kiss.

Bobby cleared his throat loudly, forcing Declan to lift his head, ending the kiss. Tess blushed and pulled out of his embrace as if she'd completely forgotten her brother was still in the room.

"I'm glad you guys have made up," Bobby

said drily. "And you've convinced me not to jump into anything, especially since my priority should be to make sure I graduate before I weigh my options."

"That's a good approach," Tess agreed.

"Absolutely. And I want you to know that Tess and I will be there to help you in any way we can," Declan added.

"Okay, great. Now can we please eat dinner?" Bobby asked with a pleading gaze. "I'm starving!"

Declan grinned and Tess broke into giggles. Even though he wanted nothing more than to discuss his future with Tess, including putting her through medical school if that was what she really wanted, he knew there was no rush.

For now, he was grateful for the precious gift he'd been given. Tess showed him the way to his faith and had offered her love.

And that was good enough for him.

# EPILOGUE

"I now pronounce you man and wife!" Pastor Tom said jovially. "Declan, you may kiss your bride."

Tess blushed as Declan bent down to kiss her, keenly aware of the fact that the entire congregation was watching them. She was thrilled that this was the first day of their new life together.

"I love you," Declan murmured as he lifted his head.

"I love you, too," she whispered back.

"We already know that," Bobby pointed out in a loud whisper. He'd stood up as Declan's best man, and she was thrilled at how her brother had turned his life around. He'd been accepted at a junior college for the next fall but had also joined the National Guard, as a reservist. It was a good compromise and she knew that Declan's influence had helped her brother make the right decisions.

"You both look so happy," Karen gushed, swiping at her eyes. Tess had asked Declan's sister to be her maid of honor, and of course Declan's twin nieces had insisted on being flower girls.

She was thrilled to have their entire family together.

"Are you ready?" Declan asked.

"Yes." She took his arm and together they walked down the aisle. He took her off to the side and gave her a big hug before the rest of the wedding party joined them in the receiving line.

"Are you sure you don't want to try to get back into medical school?" Declan asked for at least the fifth time since they'd agreed to get married. "Because I don't mind supporting you and I think you'd make a great doctor."

"I'm sure," she said. Maybe that had been her dream once, but not anymore. Maybe she'd been looking for an excuse to escape her father, too. "Declan, please believe me when I say that having a loving husband and a family is all I need to be happy."

"I promise I'll do whatever I can to make you happy." He pulled her close for another kiss, and this time, she didn't care if everyone stared at them.

This was their first day as husband and wife

And Tess was looking forward to spending the rest of her life with Declan and any children God blessed them with.

* * * * *

Dear Reader,

Welcome to my new miniseries, SWAT: Top Cops! Living in Wisconsin, I've had the unfortunate experience of two terrible mass shooting incidents in the past few years. The first was the Sikh Temple Shooting and the second was the Azana Salon Shooting. In both cases we were lucky to have an awesome response from our Milwaukee County and Waukesha County SWAT teams. Seeing these brave men and women in action as these tragedies unraveled gave me the idea to write a miniseries about them.

*Down to the Wire* is the second book in the series. Declan Shaw has a gift when it comes to defusing bombs, but when his high school crush, Tess Collins, becomes a victim of the bomber he loses his cool facade. When a second explosion nearly kills them both, it becomes clear that Tess is the target. Declan promises to do everything in his power to keep her safe, even at the risk of losing his heart. Can Tess convince Declan that he deserves to have love and a family of his own?

I hope you enjoy reading Declan and Tess' story. I'm always thrilled and honored to hear from my readers and I can be reached through my website at www.laurascottbooks.com, on Facebook at LauraScottBooks and on Twitter @laurascottbooks.

Yours in faith,
*Laura Scott*

## Questions for Discussion

1. In the beginning of the story, Tess prays for God's strength while Declan is trying to defuse the bomb. Discuss a time when you leaned on prayer especially in a time of need.

2. Tess and Declan have found each other again after ten years. They've obviously changed over time as we all do. Discuss a time when you reconnected with someone from your past and whether or not the changes you discovered were for the better.

3. Tess begins to resent Declan because he reminds her of her overbearing father. Do you think Tess is overreacting? Why or why not?

4. Tess sacrificed her dream of becoming a doctor to help raise her younger brother after their parents died. Discuss a time when you or someone you know has made a sacrifice for someone you loved.

5. Declan comes from an abusive background and doesn't think he deserves a family of his own. Discuss how faith might help Declan deal with his past in a better way.

6. Declan begins to pray when he's faced with disarming another bomb. Discuss a difficult time in your life when you turned to prayer.

7. Tess is determined to find her brother, with or without Declan's help. Discuss a time when you had to go against the people you care about in order to help someone else.

8. Declan is ready to believe the worst about Tess's younger brother, Bobby. Discuss a time when you didn't give someone the benefit of the doubt.

9. Declan learns the true meaning of prayer when he discovers Tess and Bobby have been abducted by the bomber and he's forced to make a difficult decision. Do you think he did the right thing? Why or why not?

10. Tess becomes upset when she realizes her brother may follow in Declan's footsteps. Do you think she's overreacting? Why or why not?

# LARGER-PRINT BOOKS!

## GET 2 FREE
## LARGER-PRINT NOVELS
## PLUS 2 FREE
## MYSTERY GIFTS

*Love Inspired*

### Larger-print novels are now available...

**YES!** Please send me 2 FREE LARGER-PRINT Love Inspired® novels and my 2 FREE mystery gifts (gifts are worth about $10). After receiving them, if I don't wish to receive any more books, I can return the shipping statement marked "cancel." If I don't cancel, I will receive 6 brand-new novels every month and be billed just $5.24 per book in the U.S. or $5.74 per book in Canada. That's a savings of at least 23% off the cover price. It's quite a bargain! Shipping and handling is just 50¢ per book in the U.S. and 75¢ per book in Canada.* I understand that accepting the 2 free books and gifts places me under no obligation to buy anything. I can always return a shipment and cancel at any time. Even if I never buy another book, the two free books and gifts are mine to keep forever.

122/322 IDN F49Y

| | | |
|---|---|---|
| Name | (PLEASE PRINT) | |
| Address | | Apt. # |
| City | State/Prov. | Zip/Postal Code |

Signature (if under 18, a parent or guardian must sign)

### Mail to the **Harlequin® Reader Service:**
**IN U.S.A.:** P.O. Box 1867, Buffalo, NY 14240-1867
**IN CANADA:** P.O. Box 609, Fort Erie, Ontario L2A 5X3

**Are you a current subscriber to Love Inspired books
and want to receive the larger-print edition?
Call 1-800-873-8635 or visit www.ReaderService.com.**

* Terms and prices subject to change without notice. Prices do not include applicable taxes. Sales tax applicable in N.Y. Canadian residents will be charged applicable taxes. Offer not valid in Quebec. This offer is limited to one order per household. Not valid for current subscribers to Love Inspired Larger-Print books. All orders subject to credit approval. Credit or debit balances in a customer's account(s) may be offset by any other outstanding balance owed by or to the customer. Please allow 4 to 6 weeks for delivery. Offer available while quantities last.

**Your Privacy**—The Harlequin® Reader Service is committed to protecting your privacy. Our Privacy Policy is available online at www.ReaderService.com or upon request from the Harlequin Reader Service.

We make a portion of our mailing list available to reputable third parties that offer products we believe may interest you. If you prefer that we not exchange your name with third parties, or if you wish to clarify or modify your communication preferences, please visit us at www.ReaderService.com/consumerschoice or write to us at Harlequin Reader Service Preference Service, P.O. Box 9062, Buffalo, NY 14269. Include your complete name and address.

# *Reader Service*.com

## Manage your account online!

- Review your order history
- Manage your payments
- Update your address

*We've designed
the Harlequin® Reader Service
website just for you.*

## Enjoy all the features!

- Reader excerpts from any series
- Respond to mailings and special monthly offers
- Discover new series available to you
- Browse the Bonus Bucks catalog
- Share your feedback

*Visit us at:*

**ReaderService.com**